The Birthday Stealer

By: Howard F. Razouki

Dedicated to Boumi's second generation

Chapter 1 - Many are the lights I see

Have you ever stood by the window and tried to count the millions of lights embedded across your city? Each light lighting its own story.

Ferris Bebounty used to do just that every night before his bedtime while he waiting for his mother to read him some of his favorite myths, or his father to read him an entry from his favorite book, the Encyclopedia. Ferris adopted this habit of counting city lights after he noticed how light bulbs miraculously appeared on top of the heads of his favorite cartoon characters that starred on the Super Duper Toon Time Channel. He started by counting the lights on the boats floating far across his window on Kay Bay, the giant watery mouth of the semicircular landmass area known as Kay City. Ferris also remarked how, during daytime, his home city looked like one of those giant emoticons his friends would text him. By friends he really meant his cousins Ryan and Sherry Rogers. You see, Ferris was a special kind of kid. Not in the way all parents call their kids special and not the same way his cousin Walter was special either. Ferris was born on a special day during the second most special month of the year. In school, we all learn that there are twelve months and 365 days in a year and that each month is typically 30 or 31 days with the exception of February which has 28. It's not because February is lazy or anything, but it has more to do with the way our planet rotates around the sun. Later on during school, we find out that it's takes our planet 365 and one quarter of a day. Remember, four quarters make a dollar and so every four years our planet gets one extra special day and since February could use the extra weight, especially after four years of chocolates on Valentine's Day, the calendar kings decided to tag on that extra day to February during what they call a Leap Year. Ferris was born on that fateful day, February 29th, exactly 2921 days ago. That's eight times 365 (you remember your long multiplication right?) plus one leap day. Ferris didn't like counting the quarters per year, since none of his so called school friends did. Ferris preferred to just add the extra day every four years; just like the calendar. Then again, none of his schoolmates answered in the number of days when asked how old they were. Ferris didn't know if, philosophically speaking perhaps, he was an actual eight-year-old boy or a two-year-old baby.

To make matters even more complicated, Ferris' birthday parties, whether the real one on the 29th or the fake one on the 28th were usually light in attendance. You see, the National Day and Liberation Day of Kay City fell on the 25th and 26th of February so Ferris' school typically gave the students the whole week off and families from Kay City loved to travel a lot because they loved to complain how Kay City was so very boring. Ferris knew this, because he loved counting the lights on planes just as much as he loved counting the lights on boats.

Tonight, Ferris had trouble sleeping because it was the 28th of February once again and he was three quarters of the way towards the leap day. This meant that tomorrow would be his real birthday - the 29th of February and that Ryan and Sherry would be coming over to enjoy some fancy birthday cake that his mother, Dr. May Bebounty, had bought from that store with the 31 flavors of ice cream. One for every day of the month with three extra flavors for February and only one extra for April, June, August, and November which Ferris noticed were the names of girls and female teachers in his school. All except November, which had a bakery named after it in the building where Big Uncle Murphy worked. This meant that November too was a girly name, because cakes are for girls.

Ferris never liked cake frankly. Mostly because there was always so much left over after his birthday party and we all know how bad it is to waste food. Think of all those children in Africa that don't get to eat cake or other sweets. Ferris always found that claim strange since he read in his Encyclopedia that chocolate comes from Africa. Ryan, who was chocolate colored, used to say that children in Africa and other chocolate colored children around the world don't love sweets as much as vanilla or white chocolate children.

Ryan also hated cakes and found birthdays boring. You see, Ryan was also born on a special day during a not so special month. He was born on the 21st of March - which was when Kay City celebrated Mother's Day. And while Ryan's own mother, Susan, made sure to always share the spotlight with her eldest son, Ryan always felt cheated out of his special day. He always wanted everything to be about him or about bowling.

Ferris wondered if Aunt Susan had caught any bad guys recently. You see, Aunt Susan was a police officer for the Kay City Police Department or KCPD. Ryan said she had a gun, badge, nun chucks and everything, but Ferris didn't believe the nun chuck part since Aunt Susan's nails were always so shiny and bright colored. He wondered what color they would be tomorrow during the birthday party.

Ferris also hated how his father, Dr. Hank Bebounty, would invite all his grandparents, aunties and uncles. The adult to kid ratio was totally out of whack. Plus, Ferris would have much rather had his party at Boumi's beach house. Ah yes, Boumi was what Ferris' grandmother was called, but only by Ferris, Ryan, Sherry and Sam, that is, if Sam could talk yet. You see, Boumi was not from Kay City originally and was from a place called Lux City and Sam... Sam was Ferris annoying baby brother, who seems to be sometimes from another planet altogether. Such a big baby. Born on a not so special day in a not so special month - the 17th of November. A girly month to boot.

Ferris decided to stop his counting for the night. He had barely reached above 3,000 and was nowhere near his record of 11,347. No more counting sheep either tonight. Ferris decided to simply close his eyes and keep his mind blank. He would let the empty blackness of his mind surround him and spill out into his bed, cover his room, the living room, Sam's room, his parents room, the entire apartment, the entire building, the entire block until the blackness covered the whole neighborhood. There would be no lights on tonight in this part of Kay City.

Chapter 2 - The Birthday Boy

Aunt Susan had decided to paint her nails bright pink with white waves. Ferris remarked at how they complimented the sugar frosted pink cupcakes Aunt Susan and Uncle Michael brought with them.

"Hello cousin. Happy real birthday." Whispered Ryan who was being choked by a pink with white polka dot bowtie

"Happy birthday Ferris." Greeted Sherry which was followed by a failed attempt to kiss Ferris on the cheek. Ferris was an expert at darting girly kisses, but was not so lucky when his aunties pinched and squeezed his cheeks. *Why do adults always bite and suck children's cheeks?* Ferris was still trying to figure that one out.

Uncle Michael was dressed in his usual sports shoes, sports shorts and sports shirt. Uncle Michael or Coach Mike as all the other kids had to call him during swimming practice was the only one of Ferris' uncles still involved in the most boring sport on earth. Ferris, Ryan and Sherry all hated how their parents forced them to do laps in the pool every day after school. Ferris once overheard Uncle Mike mention that soon they would have to wake up to go morning swim practice if they really wanted to become champion swimmers like him and their other uncles. Ferris shuddered at the thought, it was always so dark when he first woke up and how could they call it morning practice if he had to wake up before the sun even woke up.

"Hey there birthday boy, ready for your birthday swim today? You better eat a lot of cake; you're going to need the fuel!" Silly uncle Michael, didn't he know that food was not the same as fuel. Fuel was for mechanical things like boats and cars or trains and airplanes. Kids ate food not fuel.

The door suddenly burst open like a giant bag of popcorn that had popped its last pop. In torpedoed uncle Mitchell.

"Fesssiiiiiii."

"Uh oh...it's Crazy Uncle Mitchell" warned Ryan.

"What time is is?" yelled their over-excited uncle. Both Ferris and Ryan knew immediately what was coming next. For the question "what time is it" was not a real question, especially since Uncle Mitchell was so fond of expensive watches. It was, what Auntie Abigail once explained as rhetorical which means that it's kind of like a joke or time filler in between sentences since the person asking the question actually already knows the answer. Aunt Abigail was very smart and also taught English at Ferris school. She was also smart because she married Big Uncle. At least that's what Big Uncle always claimed.

"It's tickle time!!!!!"

With this announcement Uncle Mitchell quickly darted towards all the kids in the room, scooped them up one by one and then simply piled them one on top of the other. Ferris wondered why he was always stuck on the bottom of the pile. Uncle Mitchell would them compose himself like a masterful musician about to play the piano and then start to tickle the mountain made of children while reciting the word "Electricity....electricity" over and over again, emphasizing each syllable rhythmically, until he was either out of breath or stopped by a sane adult.

Uncle Mitchell was also known as "Apple Head." Ferris found this out from Big Uncle Murphy. Apparently Ferris' uncles also had a Crazy Uncle growing up. His name was

Monroe which was the same name as Uncle Monroe, Ferris' cool uncle who was a great artist and photographer. Uncle Mitchell though was by far the most annoying of all the uncles.

"Fesssiiiiiiii....get over here! I got a present for you."

"Mitchell stop annoying him, it's his birthday darling." That was Auntie Vanessa. She wasn't from Kay City and came from an important country that was shaped like a shoe and a sinking city by the sea. Auntie Vanessa says that her country invented pizza so that's why her country must be important.

"Sir Fesssiiiiii...do you want your birthday present or not?" Uncle Mitchell loved calling him Sir and Mister which Ferris found strange, since that in school they learned that they must use titles like sir or mister when speaking with strangers - it was called being polite. But Uncle Mitchell wasn't a stranger. He was his middle uncle right between Uncle Michael and his own mom, Dr. May.

And yes, all Ferris' uncles had names that began with the letter M. It was because Grandpa and Boumis names both began with the letter M, Moses and Mary and they decided to create an 'M-pire.' So, so far, we've met, Big Uncle Murphy, Uncle Michael or Coach Mike, and Crazy Uncle Mitchell. Then comes Fat Uncle Mark, who is a master chef and Cool Uncle Monroe, the artist/photographer.

"Sir Fesssiiii. I have summoned you. Come forth or face dire consequences" hissed Crazy Uncle Mitchell.
"Yes uncle."

"Check it out hombre. A nice giant box. I wonder what can be inside?"

"I don't know Uncle Mitchell; I don't have x-ray vision"

"Why not! Vanessa honey, remind me to schedule the X ray vision operation for Ferris immediately after his swimming practice tonight!"

"Uncle don't be silly. There is no such thing as x-ray vision in real life...it's just for superheroes in comic books and movies"

"Of course there is. I have it. Does...does that make me a superhero then?"

"Supero zero maybe." That was Aunt Vanessa. Ferris wouldn't dare insult his uncle. He had manors.
"For example, I can see what color underwear you are wearing my love." A retort snorted back right between the eyes. "Want me to prove it?"

Ferris sensed another tickle time coming up, only this time it was directed at his Aunt Vanessa. Luckily she sensed it too and casually escaped to go say hello to Auntie Abigail which solved her potential problem and created a new one for poor old Ferris. It was his real birthday after all.

"Open it." Ordered the crazy uncle as Ferris quickly tore away the shiny green gift wrap. Ferris wondered why were there were red Christmas trees sprinkled across the wrapping paper? It was February after all. Ferris casted all questions aside and opened the big brown box slowly.

"It's another box." Ferris frowned as he held a blue box with white snowmen on it.

"Open it." Ordered Uncle Mitchell once again, this time his voice had more venom in it.

Ferris obliged and rapidly tore away the blue paper and out popped another. smaller, brown box

"Oh look. It's another box." cheered Ferris sarcastically. This one was wrapped in yellow gift wrap paper with purple umbrellas.

"Well don't just stand there with that dumb look on your face mister. Open it."

Ferris could feel Ryan and Sherry watching him. He felt like a prisoner walking the pirate's plank. Ferris slowly started to shred away the yellow gift wrapping paper and surely enough there was another even smaller boring brown box hidden underneath.

Ferris looked up and saw uncle Mitchell smiling widely and wildly.

"Don't give up now Sir Ferris. You're almost there."

Sensing the end of the charade. Ferris excitedly popped open the small brown box.
No smaller box this time. There was some air inside and a rumbling sound rolling around inside the box. Ferris dunked his arm in and started searching for the buried

treasure within. His fingers felt something very strange indeed, it was both solid and slippery.

Ferris then pulled out a big bar of soap. The image sent Crazy Uncle Mitchell spiraling into a maniacal fit of loud, deafening, laughter.

"That's enough Mitchell." It was Big Uncle Murphy. "Don't you know that it's Ferris' real birthday this year. He deserves a real gift"

"Thanks Buncle." It was what Big Uncle Murphy liked to be called by his nephews. Ferris noted that he also liked it when his brothers called him Big Bro.

“Now come over here Ferris and show your buncle how bears hug.”

Immediately Ferris’ mouth began to morph into a smile. He started to growl, softly and ceremoniously, before skipping over and clamping his two skinny arms around Uncle Murphy’s chest as his buncle boosted him up towards the sky. They then both growled ferociously towards the ceiling.

Chapter 3 - Ice Cream Cake

One of the few things Ferris was looking forward to on his real birthday was blowing out the candles on his cake. For once, (well actually the second time in his short history on the planet, but certainly for the first time he could remember), Ferris Bebounty would be blowing out the correct number of candles on his birthday cake. Now that buncle Murphy had finally arrived it was time for the families Rogers and Bebounty to gather around the ice cream cake, which Ferris hoped had not melted away.

"Want me to blow them for you?" inquired Ryan as he nudged his way next to Ferris. The photo drone was buzzing getting ready to take flight from the outstretched hand of Uncle Monroe, who was usually designated as the official photographer during important family festivities. Ferris preferred the perspective of his Uncle Murphy, whose secretive snaps provided a more honest recollections of memories gone by. Ferris remembered spending many an afternoon nestled in the nook created by the arching of Uncle Murphy's rib cage and broad shoulders, captivated by picture, videos and augmented realities of him growing up.

"Waaaaaiiiiiit" wailed Crazy Uncle Mitchell. "Someone turn off the lights."

That task was delegated to Sherry, Ryan's the temperamental five-year-old sister. Undoubtedly, Sherry commanded a strong presence and carried herself with an air of authoritative contempt for anyone in her way. As the only girl of the next generation of Rogers and Bebounty, Sherry knew that she could get away with murder. Perhaps that's why she was so fond of fixating murderous glances on both her elder brother Ryan and cousin Ferris.

"Why does your sister always knife stare me?" asked Ferris

"Don't mind her cuz. Just remember to smile for the drone or your mom will make us sing happy birthday all over again."

Ryan wasn't kidding either. Ferris shivered at the thought, especially since his last (untrue) birthday was marred by a repeat of the birthday song. You see, Ferris' front teeth had not fully come out yet, forcing him to hide his fenestrated smile. This year would be different. Both his front teeth were bunny out and squeezed front and center right below a recent addition to his face that had provided his so called friends at school with endless ways to poke fun at him - they called him Ferris Four Eyes.

"Happy Birthday to You." The song had begun and as the two families sang the hearty chorus, Ryan decided to play the pinching game with Ferris, it was a game that was immensely more fun when all the adults in the room were staring straight at them.

"Ryan!" Hissed Aunt Susan. Her knife stare was all the follow up Ryan needed to cease and desist his pinching spree. It was also immediately apparent to Ferris where Sherry got her knife stare from.

"Happy birthday dear Feeesiiiii." It seemed Crazy Uncle Mitchell's moniker had caught on much to the chagrin of the Rogers and Big Uncle Murphy, who allowed the charge to go unnoticed but acknowledged his disapproval with a curt glare and casual shake of the head aimed at the source of the mischievous mondegreen.

"Happy birthday to..."

As the song came crashing down. Ferris savored the moment.

"I got this" he whispered across to Ryan. "But you can help if you like"

Ferris was sure that the two central red candles were the sort that would keep on reigniting. He remembered them from his 6th and 7th untrue birthdays. The others six white candle would surely blow out in a cinch. Ferris then began to wonder if the two red trick candles signified his second real birthday.

Thunderous bolts of laughter and clapping filled the Roger's drawing room as Ferris and Ryan unleashed the winds of triumph and truth down on the eight enemy candles. Surely enough, the two red belligerents were of the pesky variety. Ferris focused his attention on the center while Ryan decided to spray his blows from side to side. The tactic proved a resounding success as the flames were extinguished within the few seconds that Dr. May Bebounty made her way across the table to assume her central role of to cake cutter. She was a trained surgeon after all.

"Ice scream. I scream. We scream for Ice cream." Uncle Mitchell was trying to steal the spotlight once again.

"Now that's quite enough Mitchello." Barked Uncle Michael. "You're clowning around is starting to get more and more annoying." It seemed that the tide was slowly turning in Ferris' favor as the rest of the family concurred, save for Aunt Vanessa, who was too busy snickering at the ape like antics of her husband.

Uncle Mitchell puffed up his chest in a peacock like manner as he started to strut to the center of the table.

"What's the matter birthday boy? Turn that frown upside down your brown uncle just called me a clown. Go then eat your stupid cake."

Ferris tried his best to control his emotions but the pressure was too great. Just as his nose began to twitch and eyes began to itch, his cousin Ryan that came to his rescue.

"Uncle Mitchell what's that behind you?"

"What?" Exclaimed the craziest uncle, as he quickly turned backwards and then back again forwards towards the head of the table.

"This!" And with that Ryan catapulted a freshly cut piece of cake right into the face of Crazy Uncle Mitchell.

Chapter 4 - All You Have to Do is Believe

A week had barely passed and the families were now busy planning the next birthday in line - Ryan's seventh, which was due to occur in just over a fortnight. It was another lazy weekend at the Rogers beach house, Ferris and Ryan finally found themselves alone as the adults were too food comatosed thanks to another late night feast of Uncle Mark's famous barbeque.

"Good for them. I don't think I'll be going." Growled Ryan who had been in a very grouchy mood of late given what he considered to be an unfair punishment for bashing his uncle's face with birthday cake. It took all the strength of uncle Murphy and uncle Mark to hold back a rabid uncle Mitchell, the aunts had had an equally difficult time holding back their laughter.

"Are you serious? You mean you're ditching your own birthday?" Ferris asked as he tore his face away from his tablet and adjusted his glasses. Ryan noticed how his cousin sometimes did this as if it was a way for him to rewind what had just happened. Or did Ferris mistakenly think that sight and sound were somehow connected? Whichever was the case, Ryan decided to reaffirm his commitment with a more dramatic repeat.

“Yes, I said that I’m not going to my own birthday party this month. Aren't you sick of all this birthday stuff. Sure there's cake and plenty of presents, and mind you I do love a good food fight as well. I mean, that’s all nice but let's face it Ferris, birthdays in this family suck. You and I don't have any of our friends from school come over due to this stupid spring break. It’s an adult only show I tell you. They don't care about us."

"Well at least you have friends at school and at least you get a real birthday every year."

"A birthday I share with my mother's day. You've seen how everyone else in the family is so afraid of her. You think my dad cares more about me or about my mom. She has a gun remember."

Ferris knew that Ryan was right. He paused for thought before biting the bait.

"Alright Ryan, what do you think Aunt Susan will do to you when she finds out that you decided to skip your own birthday?"

"It doesn't matter. I plan to escape to Super Duper Land."

"Super Duper what?" Ferris knew exactly what Ryan had said, he just couldn't believe his ears. "You mean the place you showed me yesterday online?"

"Yes." Answered Ryan profoundly.

"But, don't you know it's make believe?"

"No cousin, don't you know that all you have to do is believe."

"Believe in what. It's a website you designed together with uncle Monroe based on the Super Duper Toon Time Channel. It's not real."

"It's more real than this dump. Plus, I have to find the Annonovosaurus and you're coming with me."

Ferris didn't know which part troubled him more. The part about leaving Kay City or the part about finding something called an *annonovowhatnow*. Ferris bit harder on the bait and Ryan knew he was reeling him in.

"Wait, what, no way. I'm not leaving. Your mom might have a gun but my mom knows karate. She's gonna chop me to pieces. And what's an *annosaurus*?"

"*Annonovosaurus*"

"Yes, that, whatever. What is it?"

"He's not a what, he's a who."

"Ok, who is this Annonovosaurus and how the heck are you going to download yourself onto the web"

"Silly Ferret. Everybody knows you upload yourself to the world wide web. Downloads are for songs, videos and virtual realities. Anyways, you especially need to meet Mr. Alberti. Apparently your birthday is the most valuable type of birthday there is."

Ferris could now feel the sweat streak across the small of his back. His heart was palpitating furiously and more and more questions began to swirl around in his head. Who is Mr. Alberti, what is an Annonovosaurus and how is his cousin seriously talking about uploading himself onto the internet?

"Ryan, are you feeling ok?"

"Of course Ferris. I'm just going over my plan in my head"

"The plan to upload yourself to the internet."
"Yup. And its to upload the both of us. Did you know that you get cookies every time you visit a website? I think I've finally figured out a way to get us up into the cloud."

Ferris heart skipped a beat. Clouds, cookies, his cousin had finally gone cuckoo.

"Ummm...I think I'm going to call my mum. You're not feeling well or you've lost your marbles Ryan."

"Don't you dare. Plus, Buncle Murphy says that Aunt May is not a real doctor and if anything is really wrong we have to see Uncle Benjamin. Uncle Benjamin is a real doctor because he studied eternal medicine which means he knows how to make you better forever."

"Ok, let's get Aunt Abigail to call Uncle Benjamin for you. Are you feeling queasy? Maybe you had too much ice tea? Remember how funny we felt after we drank some of crazy uncle Mitchell's ice tea once?"

"No I'm fine. Plus, this time it's different. I can see everything so clearly now. Get ready for the ride of your life cousin. But first, we have to find some bubble gum."

Chapter 5 - The Gum Hunter

Ferris' attempts at waking up one of the adults were continuously thwarted by his crazed cousin. Was Ryan slowly turning into the crazy uncle of their generation? Was he following in the footsteps of uncle Mitchell and his uncle before him? Ryan had certainly been acting crazy ever since Aunt Susan punished him by taking away his Wi-Fi privileges for a week thanks to his cake in the face catapult. A no Wi-Fi week was considered capital punishment to all the kids of families Rogers and Bebounty.

It seemed to Ferris that in the first day since Ryan's internet embargo had been lifted, his cousin had now officially overdosed online.

"Don't just stand there, help me find her keys."

Ryan's quest for bubble gum had led the pair across a laborious path from room to room and pocket to pocket. Ferris knew that Aunt Vanessa was very fond of chewing bubble gum, but stealing her keys and breaking into her car, especially after what Ryan had done to her husband, was certainly the most treasonous of tasks. Ferris shuddered at the thought of what torturous punishment they would have to face if caught.

Not if, but when they would be caught.

Ryan seemed to have forgotten that Buncle Murphy had rigged every room in the beach house with hidden cameras; his eyes as he liked to call them. Big brother and big uncle was always watching. *Did Ryan not care of getting caught?*

"Found them. Now quickly to the car, we haven't got much time."

This troubled Ferris further. So now there was some imaginary deadline as well. His cousin was getting crazier and crazier and he was getting worrier and worrier. *Ok Ms. Abigail. He was getting more worried!*

As they raced across the living room and down the first floor staircase, Ferris noticed how much faster Ryan was as he slid down the long polished banister. Ferris froze midway through the doorway, as he witnessed Ryan clicking open Aunt Vanessa's car's front door. Ryan dove straight in. Ferris couldn't breathe. He nervously scoured the backyard of the beach house and the surrounding parked cars for any movement.

"Good idea Ferret." Encouraged Ryan. "You play look out while I find the bubble gum."

Play? Was this all just a game to him. Didn't Ryan realize that they could get caught at any moment and that they would never be able to log on to the internet for months let alone find a way to upload themselves to the world wide web.

"Found some. Its grape flavor, but that should work just fine. Hurry, we haven't got the time."

Just then, a familiar feminine yet authoritative voice eked through.

"What are you boys doing?"

Chapter 6 - The Gum Hunter Take Two

Ferris almost fainted.

The look of astonished bewilderment on Ryan's face meant that they had been finally caught. Their foiled bubble gum caper would have certainly resulted in the both of them being punished beyond belief.

"Oh, hi Sherry." Ryan's tone was calm. "Just getting some gum."

"Does Auntie Vanessa know that you're stealing her car?" Sherry had one of her knife stares sunk in. She was strangling her stuffed uni-rabbit (that's a rabbit with a horn in the middle of its head) with equal menace.

"Shaddap up sis. We're not stealing anything." blurted Ryan with three packs of gum in his hand.

"Well you can't exactly borrow bubble gum. That's gross."

"You're gross. Now get out of our way. We have important boys only work to discuss. Come on Ferris. Let's blow this popsicle stand."

With that Ryan darted back into the beach house and marched straight into the large living room by the sea. Ferris marveled at how blue the water looked on this deranged morning.

"So... have you ever heard of smile time?" Asked Ryan.

"What, you mean like at the dentist?" Responded Ferris.

Ryan slapped his forehead in a sign of disbelief.
"No. Must I teach you everything dear cousin? Look at the clock over there."

Ferris followed Ryan's outstretched index finger towards a yellow rimmed, black faced clock hanging by the kitchen sink. The clock had red hands that looked like strings of strawberry candy.

"Ok...I'm looking," responded the bewildered Ferris. He was beginning to get slightly more annoyed than afraid. All this sneaking around and now this clockwork condescension was starting to tick him off.

"*Marshmellous*. You see how the clock looks like a smiley face almost. It's not quite 10:10 yet, but imagine if both the big hand and the little hand were both at 10...then it would look like the clock was smiling right? Uncle Monroe says that they use it in all the watch ads."

The clock was closer to 955 than 1010, but Ferris allowed his imagination to push both hands of the clock towards a number 10. Surely enough, the clock began to smile wildly.

"You're right Ryan, I see it now."

"Good, so looks like we barely have 15 minutes to practice"

"Practice what?"

"Blowing bubbles of course. Here you go. We only have one and a half packs each, so make 'em count."

Ryan tossed half a pack of gum towards Ferris and then began to devour three pieces of bubble gum all at once.

"Go on, start chewing," Ryan ordered from behind a mouthful of pinkish purple chew strings.

Ferris unfolded the packaging around the first piece. The gum felt soft, squishy and sticky between his thumb and middle finger. The day was turning out to be a humid one. He bit on it hard only to find out that the gum did not feel as soft inside his mouth as it somehow slipped across his side teeth and landed smack dab in the gap left by his two front teeth.

"Awwwwch"

"What?" enquired Ryan. His mouth still very much stuck together due to the large swaths of bubblegum sloshing around inside.
"This is rock gum. My gums hurt"

"Chew using your side teeth silly. Come on. We haven't got much time."

Ferris began to frantically chew as Ryan skipped around the living room. What was he looking for now?

"Have you see the remote?"

Ferris had just popped in his second piece of gum. This time he made sure to slay the morsel and grind it thoroughly with his back teeth before allowing it to freely swish around and mix in with the first piece.

"No." Ferris could barely speak with all the gum in his mouth. He wondered how Ryan was able to talk with half the world's gum in his. Then again, Ryan always did have a big mouth.

"Dang...why can't you ever find the remote when you need it. Alrighty then. We're gonna have to do this...as Crazy Uncle Mitchell would say...old school."

Ryan turned on the TV by flicking a switch on the back of the screen. He frantically began pressing the buttons as the bring green numbers of the screen and began climbing up the channels until finally reaching number 10. Ferris noticed how the screen remained bright blue throughout the exercise, brighter than the water from the bay.

"Why aren't there any channels on?"

"Because silly Ferret. We're using the Smart TV's 4K connectivity to the internet to fly in"

4K what? Ferris felt he knew where this conversation was heading.

"You mean this TV is connected to the internet?"

"Of course. Uncle Murphy loves his TV. Aren't all your TVs at home smart?"

Ferris deflected that question immediately. The truth was that it was the first time he had ever heard of a TV that was connected to the internet. Ferris looked back at Ryan, who was now wearing swimming goggles strapped around an outsized elite swim team swimming cap.

"And dare I ask what are those for?" Asked Ferris.

"Just in case" replied Ryan casually.

"Just in case...what?"

"Just in case the bubble pops. Don't want to get gum in my hair."

Ferris felt that his cousin was making a good point, what with all the gum swishing around in their mouths, but he was still so very unsure about why in God's name they were chewing so much gum in the first place.
“Now, how good are you at blowing bubbles?”

“Slicker than your average,” Ferris had no idea what that meant, but he had once heard uncle Murphy boasting about to his other uncles during one of their weekly card games.

“OK, so listen up, here’s the plan. At 10:10 we will have 60 seconds to blow the biggest bubble possible, we must then pull the bubble over us and then bounce into the TV.” Ryan stated nonchalantly.

Ferris stared at Ryan intently. His four eyes were transfixed on the young boy Rogers for what seemed like an eternity.

“You’re kidding me right?”

Ryan was dead serious. “No. Come on Ferret. Start blowing and start believing!”

With that Ryan began to huff and puff, sticking piece after piece of gum into his mouth as the clock ticked closer and closer to the coveted smile time.

Ferris was now hyperventilating, but quickly decided to turn his fear to his advantage. His rapid and panicked outbursts were the perfect puffs he needed to blow the biggest bubble he had ever blown.

“That’s it cousin, quick and rapid bursts of air. Rapido, rapido, rapido.” yelled Ryan followed by his customary crazed shriek of excitement.

Surely enough, both bubble buckaroos had generated giant globules of gum right in front of them.

“Now just push your head through the opening, hurry, we haven’t got the time. It’s already 10:10 and then some,” hummed Ryan from behind his giant purple bubble.

“What, no way, I... I can’t do it.”

“Believe cousin...just believe...” and surely enough, Ryan popped his head into his massive gob-glob and pulled it around the rest of his body.

Ferris was flabbergasted.

“Come on Ferris. You can do it, see you on the flip side!” yelled Ryan as he slowly bounced towards the TV.

Ferris glanced over at the clock, it seemed to him that the seconds hand was ticking at an even more hurried pace now that smile time had finally arrived. He knew it was now or never. Ferris nudged his face upwards into the giant gum sphere, he could feel his cheeks massaged by the glutinous walls as his nostrils were filled with the sweet smell of artificial grape flavoring. Through the purple haze, Ferris witnessed a spectacle that would have made him pinch himself were his arms not restricted by his wriggling into the bubble, Ryan had actually bounced into the TV.

Holy cannoli, thought Ferris. *Believe, believe, believe.*

Fully shielded within the bubble, Ferris closed his eyes, only to suddenly lose his footing.

Uh oh.

Thankfully, his trip had caused enough momentum to snowball him towards the TV. Ferris then slowly rolled and bounced into the blue screen, just a few seconds before 10:11am.

Chapter 7 - Bubble Gum City

It was a cacophony of delicious chaos. Ferris, who had barely gotten over his trans-dimensional tumult through the television, was absolutely bewildered by the spectacle in from of him. There were smartly dressed birds and giant bees buzzing about everywhere. Ferris tried his best to look beyond the commotion. In the distance, his tired eyes lighted up with the sight of the candied skyline of Bubble Gum City, capital of Super Duper Land.

"Over here cousin!" yelled Ryan. "Glad you made it through."

Ferris was too dumbstruck to answer as he slowly shuffled his way towards his cousin, who was still wearing his swim cap and goggles.

"Welcome to Sweet Port BCG, passports please." It was one of the bees and boy was it big. Ferris noticed that it was wearing the same sunglasses that Uncle Monroe was so fond off. *Annihilator...no wait, Aviator shades.*

"Right...here you go," replied Ryan as he handed the fuzzy yellow and black striped drone two ripped pages with crayon all over them. "Bees can't read," he whispered. "But they pretend to," he added.

To Ryan's surprise, the bee pulled out a scanner and ran it over the makeshift documents.

"Eh hem," grunted the bee, motioning for Ryan to remove his swim cap and goggles.

“Whoops, yup, here you go,” mumbled the young Rogers as he tore off his goggles and cap. Due to his close proximity to his cousin, more out of fear than camaraderie, Ferris heard the swim cap make a large SMACK as it almost slapped him in the face.

“Yo Ryan, be careful with that thing.”

“Shhh cuz.... don’t distract the officer.”

“Non-admissible,” droned the drone, “Rejected Entry.”

“Now hold on, wait just one second,” Ryan retorted with a newfound sense of authority. “Hold onto your horses, these documents are perfectly fine, see, its your scanner that's busted. I’ll have to speak with the Mayor about this.”

“What seems to be the problem here?” gasped a giant goose in a deep goosey voice. Ferris noticed that the voice was womanly and quite out of proportion to the sight in front of him. The lady goose was almost twice the size of the Bebounty boy wonder. Her face was covered by strange circular glasses that seemed to curve outwards forever. The goose’s pear shaped frame was accentuated by a silly little black bowler hat and vest ensemble. She went on to honk: “Visitors from the Dum Dum World are not allowed to harass our hard working waxy workers.”

Dum Dum World was what the citizens of Super Duper Land called the world from which Ferris and Ryan had come. Ferris still couldn’t believe his eyes and ears. A bee with a scanner, a goose that spoke, he was surely dreaming.

“Mr. Bumble over here is having a laugh. Now, I’m not *insectist*, but I would much rather one of the birds process our papers.” Ferris knew that Ryan had a natural knack for getting out of the stickiest of situations, but between the big bee and the giant goose, Ferris couldn’t help but feel a tad bit disconcerted.

“Well, Master...let’s see here...Master Ryar…”

“It’s Ryan”

“Oh, that’s an N is it, very well, Master Ryan, you seem to have downloaded the wrong access form. Did you visit http://www.bcgvisaforms.com/boys/names/ryanwithann.php?

“Yes.” Ferris knew Ryan was playing the goose for a hen.

“Then why does the QSR code not correspond with the internal setting of our new scanners? We just had them shipped in from Techina.”

“I don’t know, not my problem, and we have urgent business outside of the city, so it's best you don’t hold us up, or the Mayor will hear about this I promise you.”

“Very well...Officer Hiver please deliver these two gentlemen to the Mayor's office immediately. I am sure she will be able to sort things out directly. Have a good day Master Ryan with an N.”

Chapter 8 - The Mayor of Bubble Gum City

Ms. Isabelle Hicks was a tall beautiful blonde mare. As the mayor of Super Duper Lands largest city, it was a small wonder that she barely had anytime to keep up her impeccable taste in fashion. On this not so surprisingly extra hectic day, Mayor Hicks was wearing a green woven coat that smelled of spearmint. Her long neck was adorned by a bright pearl necklace and her hind legs were covered by tapered black pants that matched her hoofs perfectly. Mayor Hicks took a second to look down towards the well-kept parquet floor.

“Mrs. Coconut, call up the salon and schedule me a mani pedi,” Isabelle paused to take a quick glimpse of herself in the mirror. “Actually, make that a mani pedi and a quick B&B.”

“B&B?” enquired Mrs. Coconut. She was hard of hearing and a bit unlucky in the memory department as well.

“Brush and Blow Dry Mrs. Coconut, goodness gracious me, how many times must I repeat myself.”

“Oh, my apologies love, my hearing isn’t what it used to be...sorry. Now, I have two young lads here to see you about some mix up at the Sweet Port. They have been referred by Mrs. Gaggle. The names are Masters Ryar Rogers and Ferris Bebounty.”

“That’s Major Commando Mega Jumbo Razzmatazz,” blurted out Ryan. Ferris was too stupefied by the sight of a horse with a caramel colored mane standing upright next to a small white haired coconut in a dress, a coconut with little fuzzy arms and little fuzzy legs, standing knee up by her side. The duo from the Dum Dum world had also just passed a penguin at a desk, and two serious looking flamingo sentinels standing guard outside the Mayor's office.

"Major Commando Mega Jumbo.... well of course, please please....do sit down good sir," ushered Ms. Hicks.

"What's all this major commando stuff Ryan...what on earth are you talking about?" Ferris was deeply puzzle and on his last nerve.

"It's my Super Duper name, forgot to tell you, it's like a nom dragee, you know, like those small Mintos your dad loves to chew on."

"OK, so what's my Super Duper name then?"

"I don't know silly, you just have to come up with something, just fire up that imagination of yours."

Ferris felt threatened, he was always good at imagining things, but that always felt so very difficult when he asked to do it on the spot.

"I can't imagine anything right now, I still can't believe where we are and how we got here! Just pick something for me already."

"Ehem." Ms. Isabelle was visibly getting impatient. "Gentlemen, would you both please come closer and take a seat."

"Hold on to your…" Ryan caught himself just in the nick of time. "My cousin the fearless Sir Ferris Four Eyes the Furious of House Bebounty First of His Name and I were just preparing our official complaint."

"Honorable Major Commando Ryan…" began the mayor.

"It's Major Commando Mega Jumbo," corrected Ryan.

"Yes yes, of course, Major Commando Mega Jumbo and Sir Ferris…" Ms. Isabelle was struggling to recollect.

"Go on, state your name cousin." Ryan was trying his best to encourage Ferris, who was more fearful than fearless as his nom dragee suggested, the latter-day brave knight of Bebounty could not find the right combination of words.

"It's the Fearless Sir Ferris Four Eyes the Furious of House Bebounty, First of His Name," blurted out Mrs. Coconut

The Mayor turned her head and expressed an astonished look at the little round coco. "Very good Mrs. Coconut."

"Told ya, my memory isn't what it used to be."

"Enough with the pleasantries," Ryan had assumed his role as the aggressor. It was his go-to-move whenever he was caught in slap dab in the middle of trouble. The best defense, he had learned from his father Coach Mike, is a great offense. "I am sick and tired of being treated this way every time I decide to come take time out of my busy schedule and stopover in Bubblegum City. We have urgent business in Super Duper Land. Next time, I will refuse to enter via the Sweet Port and instead choose to enter via the Lollipolis Station."

Ferris didn't know this, but Lollipolis was the great city rival of Bubble Gum City, it was the greatest city rivalry in all of Super Duper Land. Ryan, however, was an expert in finding the right pressure points to squeeze on.

"Major Commando Mega Jumbo, on behalf of the great city of BGC, I graciously and most humbly extend our apologies. Mrs. Coconut, please see to it that these two gentlemen's paperwork is in order. I am assuming you are here to see Mr. Annonovosaurus?"

"You assume correctly your honor...we will be needing transportation arrangements as well."

"Of course, will the Pachyderm Express do?"

"It will make do," replied Ryan wryly. "We will also need two exit stamps to Annonovoburg."

"Done and done," replied the mayor curtly.

"Ms. Mayor, there is someone else here as well, she says she is with these two gentlemen." alerted Mrs. Coconut.

She? Ferris exchanged looks with Ryan. Major Commando Mega Jumbo seemed equally puzzled. They both wondered whom it may be.

"Very well, send her in," declared the Mayor.

Ferris immediately noticed the stuffed uni-rabbit.

“Hello boys, fancy fancy fancy.”

Gulp!

Chapter 9 - The Pachyderm Express

The Pachyderm Express wasn't the fastest way to get around Super Duper Land, but it was certainly the most regal. Ryan had opted for a Rhino XL while Ferris chose the Elephant MG model. The unexpected guest preferred something equally rotund.

"You just had to poke your nose in where it didn't belong, didn't you sis?"

"Shut up Major Bozo, did you really think you two rusty knobs could fool me?" exclaimed Sherry the Terrible. It wasn't her real nom dragee, but Ryan had taken to calling her that ever since she was a terrible two-year-old.

"Great, just great, and now you're slowing us down because you had to pick the slowest model, no one ever chooses the Hippo LTE."

"Well, I liked it, plus it's so pretty in pink...don't ya think?"

Ryan rolled his eyes in contempt. Sherry turned to Ferris seeking a sort of canine adoration.

"So, Sir Ferris is it...did my bolts-for-brains brother trick you into coming all the way here to sell your birthday?"

What? Sell my birthday? The look on Ferris' face said what his lips couldn't muster.

"Oh, he hasn't told you...has he."

"You shut your big fat gob and stick to talking to your little bunny doll," Ryan was beginning his offense as a defense strategy.

"Is that true cousin?" Ferris felt more confused than defeated or cheated by Ryan. He was almost glad that Sherry had someone found her way into Super Duper Land, it made the adventure far more palpable, far more real.

"Alright, you got me, it was supposed to be a surprise. Ferret, you and I have been dealt what uncle Mark calls the shorthand."

My hands aren't short...are they?

"Stop looking at your hands silly, he means figuratively," zinged Sherry.

Figuratively. Ferris had remembered that word from a homework assignment that Auntie Abigail helped him with once. Something about smiling and a mosasaurs, but Ferris couldn't be bothered to think at the moment. He was suffering from a huge headache. Nevertheless, he decided to egg on the Major Commando. "OK, and what surprise is that?"

"Well, you will find out soon enough. Now, I don't know about you guys, but we're in Super Duper Land and we have yet to enjoy the fat of the land, I'm starving."

Ferris has no idea why Ryan was talking about fat, but he did feel both hungry and borderline hangry.

"Fine," mopped Ferris, "Where shall we stop to eat?"

"Just look around four eyes, anywhere we darn choose," retorted Ryan.

Ferris craned his neck slowly to his right. There was nothing but gloomy hill upon gloomy hill surrounded by a murky dark sky.

"I don't see anything appetizing anywhere," moaned the not so bright knight of Bebounty.

"That's because you have a low IQ," replied Ryan.

"What? You mean like my intelligence? I'll have you know that I got straight A's last year mister Mega Jumbo or whatever you want to call yourself."

"No my dummy from another mummy, not I as in Intelligence, I as in Imagination. Now, what did I tell you back at the beach house? Just believe. Close your eyes, take a few deep breaths, imagine, and believe."

Ferris felt suffocated. All these instructions, halve-truths and loaded promises. He felt the world closing around him as he closed his eyes as tightly as he could and began to breathe heavily, in and out, in and out.

"Cousin," Ferris could feel a soft cool grip on his arm. It was Sherry. "My dunce of a brother is right, we're actually in Super Duper Land. So turn that frown upside down and set your mind free."

“I’m trying, I swear I am, but all these bad thoughts are closing in on me. I can’t do it,” cried Ferris.

“Shhhhh,” Sherry started to speak softly. “Whenever I have a bad thought that is trying to enter my head, I just pop into a bubble and simply blow it away.”

“You can also imagine that you're at the beach. I like to put my bad thoughts on little sailboats and push them out to sea and see them rolling over the wave,” added Ryan.

“Or that,” Sherry cast a friendly yet slightly annoyed face at Ryan. “Or just do whatever works for you.”

“Well, I did blow that giant bubble on my first try. Um, how about small paper planes? I’m good at making those too.”

“Yes you are! That’s perfect!” exclaimed Ryan. “This is Problem Flight 101 paging Control Tower Central at Ferris International Airport, we have multiple flights stranded on the runway, permission to take off sir.”

Ferris opened his eyes and flashed his toothless smile. “Permission granted.”

He imagined paper plane after paper plane filled with all of his imaginary problems gusting off into the great blue beyond. Ryan and Sherry joined in the fun, making zoom-zoom noises as Ferris frantically began tossing his problems right and left, one perfectly folded paper plane after the other. Each plane transforming the land around him. Super Duper Land suddenly became brighter and far more colorful. The colors were so intense; they were dancing vividly. Ferris never knew that you could actually feel colors. He immediately noticed the cotton candy clouds, so pink and fluffy, just floating about, enjoying the cool breeze. Next, his eyes turned to the wide milky river that snaked its way across the valley, huge brown logs were floating calmly along.

Trees.

Ferris dismounted his pachyderm and walked over to the nearest edge of the vast expanse of the forest surrounding the trail. He ran his hands across the bark and could feel it's crumbliness beneath the tips of his fingers. He knew it was now or never. He now knew how to finally believe.

Ferris bent his head sideways and took a large bite out of the bark. His side teeth dug into the soft flakey chocolatey cambium. It was sweet and wholesome chocolate heaven. As the mouthful of chocolate bark slowly melted in his mouth, the curious knight of Bebounty arched his head upwards and noticed the succulent fruit of these candied trees. Plump cookies (of both the chip and sandwich variety), blueberry muffins and double chocolate brownies were suspended in a sweet symphony of baked goodness. He ravished through the branches and began picking the choicest and fattest pieces. He then quickly tossed a few over to both Ryan and Sherry, who happily devoured the melting morsels.

“Go higher Ferret!”

Ryan’s command was heard by Ferris’ elephant, who slowly marched over to his newly minted master, extending his long trunk and propelling the sweet knight of Bebounty up into the green foliage that crowned the top of the forest.

Ferris was relieved when he realized that there really were no vegetables in Super Duper Land. Upon closer inspection, he noticed that the leaves of the trees were of the gummy variety, each uniquely delectable in its own way. Ferris noticed that Sherry too had dismounted her Hippo LTE. His eyes followed her as she carried a rosy red pale towards the milky river.

“Well, we can’t have cookies without the cream,” she said with a smile as she skipped back towards her cousin.

Ferris knew that Sherry was right. He could feel the inside of his mouth getting stickier and stickier from all the chocolate and candy he was munching on. Ryan too had dismounted and joined both his sister and cousin under the shade of the chocotree. They had assembled a glorious picnic.

As he sat down in his usual frog shaped position, Ferris noticed sprouts of lollipops popping up around the tree. He quickly culled three and distributed them evenly amongst the traveling trio.

“Mine tastes like strawberry milk,” cheered Sherry. Ferris wondered if it was really strawberry milk flavored or if Sherry’s river milk run had influenced her taste buds. His lollipop, on the other hand, had a sharper, tangier taste, somewhere in between grape and kiwi, which almost raised an alarm, since Ferris had learned at an early age that he was allergic to that ugly egg shaped hairy little green fruit.

“Mine tastes like pineapple and mango,” yelled Ryan. “Good picks cousin” he added as he quickly crunched away the lollipop. *What a waste*, Ferris thought.

"You're supposed to savor it, Ryan. Lick it, suck it, not crunch it!"

"Why Sir Ferret, when we are surrounded by so many flavors, why wait silly."

Ryan did have a point, so Ferris noisily crunched away at his own kiwi grape lolly. Just as he was about to discard the stick, the Major Commando grabbed him by the wrist.

"Don't you know anything Four Eyes, you're supposed to replant them. We gotta be green, even here in Super Duper Land."

Ferris was confused but followed Ryan's lead in plugging the empty lollipop stick into the ground.

"Now if we pour some milk on them, they will most probably have a milky flavor, but just to be creative, let's plant some of these gummy leaves as well so that the flavors can have a great mix. There we go." Ryan exclaimed proudly.

"Che-kaw!"

Ferris and Ryan's attention was drawn upwards. They looked overhead, it was the fluffiest bird Ferris had ever seen.

"Oh my God, I can't believe our luck. We finally saw one," hissed Ryan in the softest voice his excitement could allow.

"What...what is it Ryan?"

“It's a Mallow Sparrow.”

“A what?”

“A Mallow Sparrow, they lay marshmallow eggs, the tastiest, fluffiest morsels you will ever eat. Here, hold my cookies, I have to go get us some!”

“Ryan, don’t be a doofus, you can’t be serious. I don’t think that you can climb that tree all on your own?” Sherry drew an immense amount of pleasure popping Ryan’s adventurous bubbles of ambition.

“Hmmm...you’re right sis, it’s way higher than the cookie brownie line.... but I have a plan. Oh Ferris?”

Ferris felt a rush of worry wash over him. What harebrained scheme did his crazy cousin just cook up? Moments later, Ferris found himself supporting the full weight of his cousin on his two shoulders. Ryan was much heavier than he was, but Ferris was too cowardly to choose the options of foraging through the Mallow Sparrow’s nest. Instead, he chose to be the bottom of the two kid tall human ladder. Well, it was actually a two kid human-elephant ladder. You see, Ryan had somehow convinced Ferris to make use of his elephant’s trunk once more, only this time, the feat would be far more circus spectacular and far more dangerous - Ryan also wanted the poor pachyderm to stand on its two hind feet in order for him to reach the treasured Mallow Sparrow’s nest.

As wobbly as it was frightening, Ryan’s plan was a success, even though it was initially stifled by the Mallow bird’s persistent pecking and screeching, a natural mechanism to defend its nest from Ryan’s intruding fingers. Alas, the poor bird was way too soft and too fluffy to do any harm, its hard-fought defensive thrusts felt like mini tickles on Ryan's hands, and although known to be extremely ticklish, the Major Commando was resistant thanks to his laser-like focus on the Mallow's eggs. Having clutched a good half dozen, Ryan somersaulted down off of Ferris' shoulders and into the nearby milk stream. His face and hair ran rich with the creamy white river milk as he triumphantly raised both his fists full of Mallow eggs in the air.

"Marshmellous," exclaimed Ryan.

Masrhmellous indeed.

Chapter 10 - Just Blaze

The trio had eaten their fill and felt re-energized, for there were no bellyaches in Super Duper Land. They had just decided to resume their course when they heard a large moan:

"Ouuuuuuuuuch."

"Shhhhh...did you guys hear that?" asked Sherry.

"Ahhah," replied Ryan nodding readily.

"I think it came from over there," suggested Ferris, pointing towards a giant orangey brown boulder. Upon closer inspection, Ferris noticed that the boulder was actually not made out of one of the three forms of rock; sedimentary, metamorphic, or igneous but a giant vanilla frosting filled pumpkin cake.

As they proceeded gingerly towards the bellowing noise, Ferris's four eyes caught sight of a slithering brown serpent.

"Jeepers a snake! "The timid first knight of Bebounty had summoned the alarm.

"Cool your jets cousin," assured Sherry, "if it was a snake, then where is its head?"

Ferris was too afraid to find out. "It's probably a super long snake hidden behind that giant cake rock."

"Silly Ferret, there are no snakes in Super Duper Land, but there are…" Ryan dismounted his Rhino and ran around right round the rock, Sherry did her best to follow suit, her stuffed uni-rabbit dragging along the grass beneath them. Ferris skewed himself wider and wider towards an angle that would slowly (and safely) revealed the source of the loud ouch sound and the slithering brown fake snake.

...Dragon!

It's skin glittered like a thousand gold coins in the Super Duper Land sunlight. Upon closer inspection, Ferris noticed that the dragon was a reddish brownish color, which reminded him of Auntie's Abigail's famous gianduja red velvet cupcakes. He also noticed how the dragon's jaw was protruding like that of a bulldog. The dragon continued to groan out loud.

"Ooooooouuuuuccchhhh!" It was obviously in tremendous pain.

"Poor dragon," consoled Ryan, "seems like you got yourself stuck in between a rock and a hard place."

Ferris watched Sherry roll her eyes in contempt before slamming her brother with the stuffed uni-rabbit.

"Ouuuuuch," the dragon bellowed once more. "I was flying low to attempt a new aerial maneuver, and my tail must have gotten stuck in that crooked crevice. That bloody thing has a mind of its own you know!"

He speaks! But then again so did all the citizens of Super Duper Land.

“Shouldn’t be a problem kind sir,” assured Ryan as he rolled up his sleeves and popped on rubber gloves and geeky eye protection plastic glasses. Ferris immediately wondered where he had pulled them out of.

“We should have you back up in the air in a jiffy,” promised Ryan.

“You are too kind young blood, what is it they call you?”

“I am Major Commando Mega Jumbo Razzmatazz, and that’s my cousin, Sir Ferris Four Eyes the Furious, Knight of Bebounty and my kid sister, Her Royal Highness Princess Her Sherryness the Terrible.

“Pleased to meet you all, ouuuuuuch,”

“Pleasure,” snorted Sherry, “but please drop the terrible added by my dimwitted brother. And you can call me Sherry Mr. Dragon.”

“Pleased to meet your acquaintance Your Highness, you may also call me if it pleases your grace, Sir Blaze Barras-Hargan. Ouuuch. Or you can just call me Sir Blaze. Ouuuuuch…. or just Blaze.”

Blaze. Now that’s a dragon’s name if I ever did hear one, and he’s a knight too, a Dragon Knight.

“But please hurry, I have been in excruciating pain this whole morning,” moaned Sir Blaze.

"We'll get right too it," assured Ryan. "Sir Ferris, with me."

Ryan skipped towards the boulder, clutched his two hands together near his pelvis, forming a large circle with his arms. He was arching his heads backwards and upwards. Ferris knew what his cousin was gesturing towards. It was the elephant escapade all over again and the Major Commando had that same crazed look on his face. Ryan wanted him to use his hands as a springboard to climb up the boulder.

"Come on Ferret, we haven't got all day!"

Ferris shook the cobwebs of fear slowly closing in on his courage. He pumped out his chest and ran over to Ryan who carefully catapulted him up onto the pumpkin cake boulder. The surface felt oddly soft, but sticky, which allowed the spider knight of Bebounty to easily climb the rest of the way up.

Not surprisingly, the top of the boulder was crusted in a thick frosting. Ferris flicked his finger through the rich creamy opacity and popped it into his mouth.

Mmmmm, vanilla.

"Stop your tasting and start chowing down cousin," yelled Ryan from below.

"What?"

"You have to eat all the cake that's around the midpoint of Sir Blaze's tail," explained Ryan.

“What, you mean all of it?”

“No you knucklehead, just enough for him to wriggle it out.”

“Just enough for it to wriggle itself out you mean,” corrected Blaze. “My tail has a mind of its own.”

“Come on Ferris, start eating!” yelled Sherry

“But I’m so full from all the cookies and chocolate eggs, I, I don’t think I have it in me.”

“If you believe it, you will achieve it, Sir Ferris,” encouraged Blaze. “I believe in you.”

Ryan and Sherry began to slowly chant: “Ferris, Ferris, Ferris.” It was a blissful soft cacophony that erupted into a rambunctious cheer once Blaze joined in as well. Ferris felt energized. He ploughed his face full on into the frosting, licking, inhaling and stuffing his cheeks with mouthfuls of delicious vanilla frosting and pumpkin cake. He was swallowing pieces hole and moving his head rapidly from side to side like the carriage of an old typewriter.

“Ouuuuuuuch!”

Oppps. Ferris tasted the sharp taste of dark chocolate. It’s bitterness and acidity mixed well with the sweetness and fullness of the cakey rock. Ferris opened his eyes to disbelief. He han taken a big bite out of Blazes tail!

Ferris wasn't exactly sure what happened next. He remembered flying through the air for a bit. He remembered the sight of the pink cotton candy clouds floating above and the sound of the boisterous milk river lapping against the banks of lollipop filled meadows. He certainly didn't remember crashing onto the ground below or getting whipped by Blaze's tail.

"Is he ok? That was quite a tumble."

"Shake him Sherry."

"No you shake him."

"What if his neck is broken?"

"Shhh, shhh, I see his eyes opening."

"My apologies Sir Ferris, I warned you, my tail really does have a mind of its own."

"Sir Blaze, why does a dragon wag its tail?" Asked Ryan so matter of factly. Ferris felt a piercing pain poke through his back.

"Well, it's because the dragon is supposedly smarter than the tail."

"Hmmm...good answer," assured Ryan. "So how come you were aerial blundering this morning?"

"Stripes," answered the dragonknight curtly.

"Pardon, come again?" It was Sherry asking this time.

""I need to earn my stripes back before I can breathe fire again." It was more of a whimper than a whine, as Blaze glanced longingly at his stripeless wings.
"You've, you've lost your fire?" Ferris finally spoke. It was as if his words had this strong magnetic quality about them as both his cousins and the dragon immediately dragged their faces down towards him. Ferris noticed how Ryan, Sherry and Blaze's heads formed an oddly shaped three leaf clover, a three leaf clover with a halo around it. Ferris wondered if it was from the trio of heads blocking the sun or from the after effects of his fall.

"He speaks!" cheered Sir Blaze. "Allow me to be of assistance my fellow knight."

Ryan felt oddly at home in Blazes arms. He was dizzy when he first stood up, but soon composed himself enough to roll his sleeves back down. Licking his lips, Ferris noticed that he still had a lot of vanilla frosting surrounding his own cake hole. He also noticed his two cousins snickering away and imagined how silly he must have looked.

"You look like a demented clown cousin with all that frosting around your mouth," chuckled Ryan.

"A cake eating clown," added Sherry.

"Well, I for one, have the honor of saluting this brave clown of cake."

Up until then, Sir Blaze had stayed mostly hunched down. It was partly due to the pain he felt in his tail and his concern for Ferris after the fall. Presently, Sir Blaze Barras-Hargan, the bulldog faced brown dragon, arched his magnificent red velvet wings upwards and outwards, pumped up his own dragon-sized chest and stretched his hind legs to their maximum upright height. He then ceremoniously brought his front right claw to his horned forehead in chivalrous salute.

"Cool," gaped Ryan widely.

"Fancy fancy fancy," stammered Sherry.

"I salute thee, Sir Ferris Four Eyes, Knight of Bebounty. For your honor, valor and service to your fellow knight." It was the infamous Super Duper Land salute.

"Here here," cheered Ryan and Sherry as each joined in step, Ryan on Blaze's right and Sherry on his left, saluting their recuperating cousin, each with their own proud rendition of the Super Duper Land salute; three middle fingers tall and firm, with a small circle formed by touching the thumb to the littlest finger.

Needless to say, this was the proudest moment in Ferris' life.

Ferris had also just realized that he was 3000 days old today, but that was back in Kay City. Today though, he was reborn as a citizen of Super Duper Land.

Chapter 11 - Yu - The First Virtue of Knighthood

As the Super Duper Land sun approached midday, our three travelers and their new friend, Sir Blaze Barras-Hargan, decided to form a pact. In exchange for their help in setting him free, the dragonknight insisted on helping the Dum Dum citizens accelerate their trip to Annonovoburg.

Ferris had finally found a way to get the rest of the frosting off of his face and Ryan had decided to send the pachyderm express packing back to Bubblegum City. They were going airborne.

Blaze had offered to fly them the rest of the way to Annonovoburg as recompense for helping him out of his sticky boulder situation. Ferris was surprised by how smooth the takeoff was and how vast the scenery of Super Duper Land was beneath them.

"So how is it that you lost your fire? I never knew that the stripes on the wing of a dragon were the fire producer," asked Ferris. They weren't flying too fast, which meant that Blaze could easily hear him.

"I'd rather not talk about it Sir Ferris, but I can promise you this. I will one day get my stripes back and that nefarious nunce of a Griffin will get his just desserts."

"What's a Griffin?" asked Sherry.

"The most treacherous beast there is your grace, foul in every way, devoid of dignity, no respect for the seven virtues knighthood."

“That’s the one that has the head of a lion and the body of a snake with wings!” blurted Ryan.

“No it's not,” corrected Ferris. “A griffin has the head and wings of an eagle, and the body and tail of a lion.”

“Indeed, such a brute and ugly beast!” added Blaze. “King of Land and Air my arse!”

“Right right right,” verified Ryan. “And its front legs are actually talents!”

“You mean talons cousin.”

“What are talons?” asked Sherry.

“Their basically the claws that all birds of prey have,” replied the knowledgeable knight of Bebounty.
“Wow, I didn’t know that birds were so religious.”

Ferris just shook his head. He was done explaining basic mythology and was more interested in something Blaze had just mentioned. The Seven Virtues of Knighthood. His cousin Ryan had casually knighted him only a few hours ago after their miraculous journey through the TV and into the Sweet Port of Bubblegum City. Ferris wondered though, what were the Seven Virtues of Knighthood, and did he, as the first knight of Bebounty, exhibit them all?

“Ummm...Sir Blaze”

“Yes, Sir Ferris.”

"Which of our seven virtues did the griffin not share?"

"All of them."

Fail. Ferris tactful inquiry had been shot down. Should he be a bit blunter with Blaze? Ferris was too ashamed to admit that he had no idea what any of the seven virtues were. He couldn't fathom the look on Sir Blaze's face if he somehow found out that Ferris was a fake knight, a boring four-eyed fraud.

"Wait, what's that down there?" screamed Sherry.

"Where...where?" asked Ryan.

"Down there in that gorge."

"What's a gorge?" asked Ryan.

"A gorge is a narrow valley between hills or mountains, typically with steep rocky walls and a stream running through it, I think the stream itself is also called a ravine," blurted out Ferris, he was glad his geography report on geological structures finally came in handy.

"A damsel in distress, we must descend," roared the Dragon Knight.

"Dive Sir Blaze, dive dive dive," charged the Major Commando.

****

Miss Amy Mone, looked like a mushroom. She even dressed like a mushroom would, in a frilly white dressed covered in red polka dots and a droopy white hat that made it look as if she was wearing a mop on her head. She had bright blue skin that was accentuated well by her blonde hair and bright red snout. She was squealing in horror when Ferris first laid his four eyes on her. He had never seen a blue pig, or better yet, a blue pig standing on two hind legs and dressed like a giant mushroom. But then again, they were in the wild wanderlust of Super Duper Land.

"Save us!" shrieked the not so attractive damsel in distress. "It has risen!"

"Fear not fair damsel," announced Sir Blaze. "We shall protect you and your fellow villagers from any threat of danger, may I introduce, Major Commando Mega Jumbo, Sir Ferris the Furious and Her Highness Princess Her Sherriness. We are at your service."

"We haven't got the time," cried out Miss Mushroom. "It's coming."

"What is coming fair damsel," asked Ryan. *Enough with the fair part*, thought Ferris.

"The Twydra."

Ferris had no idea what the poor little piggy was talking about, but he could feel the shivers running up his spine. In the distance, thundering footsteps meant that whatever this Twydra thing was, it would be big, and judging by the fear in the eyes of the hideous damsel, big and mean.

“Battle positions,” ordered Sir Blaze. “Form a line, Sir Ferris, on me.”

Battle? They were just having cookies and milk a few moments ago. Knights weren’t supposed to fight, were they? *The art of fighting without fighting.*

“But we, we, haven’t got any weapons?” tested Ferris. His shivers had shifted into shakes.

“Yes we do!” answered Ryan as he handed Ferris a golden sword. “Just be sure to check the balance cousin, and remember to step forward when you swing, put all your weight behind it. Oh, and the pointy end goes in first.”

Again with the tools, thought Ferris. Where on Earth does he carry all these items. As he tightly gripped the pommel of his sabre, Ferris admired the axe wielded by the Major Commando. It was huge. Twice the size of Ryan’s head, which had somehow found a helmet to hide in. Sherry on the other hand, wore a strange silver eye patch with a hole in it, while she straddled a quiver of steel arrows on her shoulder and bent a large wooden bow in between her hands. Her stuffed uni-rabbit was tucked neatly under her right arm as she stretched out the bow’s string.

Ferris looked up to his fellow knight. Sir Blaze was intensely focused on the forest ahead, a giant club gripped tightly in his right hand, complemented by a giant shield in his left.

Shield. I need a shield.

“No shields for us?” squeaked Ferris.

“Great idea cousin, here you go.” Ryan slowly and quietly handed Ferris a beautiful kite shaped shield, gold of course, to match his sword. Ferris noticed that Ryan had opted for a much larger shield himself. It was both oblong and convex and covered nearly almost all of Ryan’s body.

“Do you mind if I take your shield and you take mine?” peeped Ferris.
“What?” The ground beneath them was now trembling way more than Ferris’ legs were, plus, Ryan was mimicking Blaze’s laser focus at the task at hand.

“Can we switch shields cousin?”

“What, fine, sure, whatever, just keep your eyes ahead Sir Ferris. This is no time to daydream.”

Daydream. More like nightmare. For the first time since they arrived in Super Duper Land. Ferris Four Eyes Bebounty wished that he was back in Kay City, snuggled in bed, the giant family encyclopedia by his side instead of some giant red shield.

“Hold the line,” screamed Blaze. “Princess Sherry, arrows up.”

“Arrows up,” confirmed the bow-mistress.

“On my command, make it rain, three, two, one...loose.”

Ferris followed the path of the first arrow. Sherry’s aim was on point, she had let loose a barrage of arrows fired in quick succession, emptying her first quiver before Ferris could even blink. Her arrows were arching upwards and over into the most ferocious fiend Ferris had ever seen.

The Twydra was a giant lime green monster with small, shiny, salt like flecks peppered across its slimy skin. It had a wide base, four stumpy legs and nine giant serpent-like heads.

No snakes in Super Duper Land, sure, but giant monsters with nine snake heads. Sold.

To Ferris' dismay, Sherry's arrows had no effect whatsoever on the charging beast. As the Twydra scrambled towards their little armada, Ferris decided to bolt. Exit stage left. Ferris ran as fast as his legs could carry him.

"Great idea Sir Ferris, a left-flank maneuver!" cheered Sir Blaze. "Major Commando, attack the right flank and complete the double encirclement stratagem suggested by Sir Ferris. He is furious indeed, yes he is!"

Ferris heard none of that. He was too busy finding the strength and stamina to run and carry his large shield and sweat covered sword. To his horror, his escape route was cut off by a large rock wall.

A gorge is a narrow valley between hills or mountains, typically with steep rocky walls. Great, just great. It seemed that the 'flight not fight' knight of Bebounty had no choice but to get back into the heat of battle.
But the Twydra was no foolish foe. After crashing the bulk of its body into Sir Blaze's giant shield, it then completed its sordid battle stance in the middle of the square circle created by the three would be warriors and the

dragonknight, all the while hissing and spitting a strange green gooe. It had divided eight of its nine heads equally amongst our four heroes, with the central and slightly darker head spinning around, Ferris noticed how it looked as if the middle head was in charge.

“Major Commando, on my command charge the two heads on my right, slice and dice baby, slice and dice. Sir Ferris, repeat the same maneuvers on the left while I distract the middle three heads,” barked Sir Blaze.

“Roger that,” affirmed Ryan. Ferris was too terrified to acknowledge the order.

“Princess Sherry, aim for the eyes, let's see if that stops them from slithering about., on my mark comrades, 3, 2, 1. Attack!”

The arrows had a menacing impact on the Twydra's beady little eyes, if by menacing you mean infuriating the beast ever more so. Most surprisingly, even though Ryan was successful in chopping the heads off the creature from all angles, astonishingly, two new heads would sprout up in place of the severed one. The Twydra now boasted as many as 13 different heads.

“What sorcery is this?” yelled Sir Blaze is disbelief.

“We must find a way to stop them from growing,” added Ryan. “Ferris, you're the smart one, use your brain!”

Ferris was too overcome by fear to move. He had heard both Blaze and Ryan, but he felt that his tongue was frozen in its place. Once again, he knew he had to shake away those horrible cobwebs of cowardice. The time to be courageous was at hand.

“Ummmm, we, we need to seal them somehow. Blaze, you need to find your fire!”

“Fire? I can’t do it. I told you. I need to earn my stripes back.” Blaze’s temporary misdirection of focus resulted in him lowering his guard. The Twydra took full advantage of this, and managed to spray Blazes right wing with its sticky acidic green gooe.

“Ouuuuuuuch,” Blazes all too familiar bellow.

“That’s it, I’ve had it,” screamed Ryan as he charged the main body of the beast only to be scooped up by a big bite that grabbed Ryan by his kite shield, hoisting him up in the air. The Major Commando was now wriggled back and forth in a rapid whiplash like motion.

“Woooooah, woooooah, I’m going to hurl!”

And so he did, his projectile vomiting distracted the main head of the Twydra just long enough for Blaze to get out of harm's way and for Sherry to rearm her quiver, the self-proclaimed princess was probably on her fourth by now.

As for Ferris, the petrified knight of Bebounty was simply trying not to soil himself. He decided it was time to properly escape, so he sallied his shield on his back by fastening the grips tightly to his shoulders. He then ploughed his sword into the mountain’s cliff face and started climbing upwards, one jab at a time. Ferris remembered the day his Uncle Monroe had taken him and Ryan indoor rock climbing back in Kay City, there were no giant eighteen or twenty-something headed monsters back then.

"Help, it's got me, help."

Ferris recognized Sherry's voice, but he was too afraid to turn back and face the debauchery below. Out of the corner of his eye he could bare full witness to the carnage as Sir Blaze swatted away half a dozen heads with his club and battered shield. The peaky knight of Bebounty could also see both Ryan and Sherry struggling in different jaws, Ryan using his shield and Sherry using her bow as a makeshift tent poles, each propping up their own deadly Twydra mouth tent.

The Twydra hadn't forgotten Ferris though. With Blaze overwhelmed and Ryan and Sherry literally tied up, the beast turned the bulk of its focus, meaning the bulk of its heads, towards the small red shielded coleopterous child climbing the cliff ahead.

Ferris had made it halfway up the cliff, *a gorge is a narrow valley between hills or mountains, typically with steep rocky walls,* when the Twydra started to plunge head after head into the space just below him. It was a barrage of battering ram thrusts. A trembling blitz of horror that quickly had Ferris hanging by a single arm. He could feel the palms of his hands getting sweatier and sweatier as his grip on the pommel of the sword grew tighter and tighter yet somehow less and less stable at the same time. Noticing Ferris' dire strait, the Twydra decided to deliver a final coupe de grâce and hurl its entire body at the rock face below the hanging knight of Bebounty. This great burst of kinetic energy not only sent Sir Ferris flying through the air for the second time today, but also unleashed the potential energy of a group of giant boulders perched high above on the cliff's edge.

Soon after Ferris broke his fall on a bushel filled with white chocolate strawberries, the boulders proceeded to crush and bury the Twydra and its murder of heads, save for the slightly darker central one, which wriggled in severe pain and directed its last few moments of focus on the fallen knight of Bebounty.

Instinctively, Ferris raised his right arm to guard his face, only his right arm was still stuck to his golden sword, which easily sliced through the gaping mouth of the Twydra's biting head, splitting it in half and covering Ferris in super sour slime.
Smack. Smack. Were the sounds Ferris' lips made as his face puckered up like a porpoise. He recognized the tangy taste...*Lime Licorice!*

"Hoorah! Well done Sir Ferris. You are a true master of deceptive warfare. A noble knight," praised Sir Blaze.

"Yes, well done cousin, I knew you had it in you," chimed Sherry.

"Dang it Four Eyes, you know I had him, my axe game was on point, a few more slices and I would have..."

"The greatest art of war, is the art of war without war. The art of fighting without fighting." Blaze was right. Ferris had found a way to use the Twydra's own brute strength against it. "It is the central tenet of Yu."

“Ummm...thank you Sir Blaze, you're too kind, but I believe it was *you* that we all owe our thanks to, I just…” stammered the reluctant knight of Bebounty.

“Har har har.” Ferris had never seen a dragon laugh, so his immediate reaction was that Blaze was cross, not happy “A courageous and courteous knight if I ever did see one. Comedic as well, using *you* as a pun for Yu, can’t say that’s been done before,” chuckled Sir Blaze.

“Wait, I’m lost here, what’s going on?” asked Sherry.

“Sir Ferris used Yu, Y-U in the same way we use you, Y-O-U,” countered the snickering dragon.

“Ok...and?” continued Sherry

“And? Well, Ferris can explain the meaning of Yu, that’s Y-U and not Y-O-U.”

Everyone turned to Ferris. Ryan started to smirk ever so slightly. It was worse than that feeling Ferris would get when his English Teacher Mr. Steve would ask him a question in from of the whole class, a question he hadn’t the foggiest idea of how to answer.

“Alas, it seems that Sir Ferris is still caught up in the heat of battle, let me explain the difference your grace. You see Yu, Y-U or Yuuki is knightspeak for the first and perhaps the most important of our seven virtues - courage. We can all testify in truth, that courage is not the absence of fear itself, but the ability to conquer those fears when it counts. The sigil of courage is a usually misconstrued to be a big bear, but all knights know that the true symbol of Yu is the fox. Courage requires cunning more than it does brute strength or size, since one must overcome their inner fear by deceiving oneself into acting courageously, usually in the most dangerous of circumstances. Sir Ferris the Furious, you are the most fantastic of foxes. Once again, I have the honor of saluting thee. Here here!"

And with that wonderful explanation, Sir Blaze raised his mighty bruised and battered body, wincing slightly in pain as he did so. He was unable to arch out his wounded right wing, but the Super Duper Salute spectacle was far more endearing than the first. Ferris however, felt a huge lump in his throat, it was even bigger than the first one he felt after eating Sir Blaze's tail out of pumpkin cake captivity.

Gulp!

Ryan and Sherry followed suit in the salute, but with far less vigor. Ferris was sure he knew why but was too busy fending off the wet-faced onslaught of the thankful Ms. Amy Mone and the rest of the blueberry swine villagers who had also come to salute the hoaxer hero.

Chapter 12 – Meiyo

Since Sir Blaze had promised to take the trio all the way to Annonovoburg and since a knight was only as good as his word, our three travelers maintained their dragonly escort, albeit on foot. Their intended short flight across Super Duper Land had been forced into a long march. Ryan's constant glances over at Ferris made the journey feel even longer.

"You need to tell him"

"Shut up Major Bozo," whispered Ferris. "It's your fault we're in this mess."

"Well, you're the one that hates the day he was born on."

"I'm not born on a day, my birthday is every four years remember, at least you get to celebrate your real birthday every year."

"Yeah, but my Mum is the one that usually has all the fun, I..."

"Would you two please be quiet, isn't it enough that we now have to walk all the way to see the Annonovosaurus, just walk, no talk, my poor uni-rabbit has big ears you know, so spare us the moaning." Sherry was in a particularly terrible mood. Ferris couldn't care less though; he was too busy replaying the day's past events in his head. Most of all, he dreaded confronting his fellow knight.

Oh who am I kidding, I'm no real knight. I'm a nothing knight.

Suddenly, in the distance, Ferris could hear a jarring concord of shrieks.

“Eyaaaaw, eyaaaaaw!”

Why am I always the first person to sense danger?

“Did you guys hear that?”

“That I did Sir Ferris, cast your eyes there, towards the horizon.”

Ferris squinted and noticed a small inverted V heading towards them at an alarming pace.

“Battle positions?” enquired Ryan.
“Yes Major Commando Mega Jumbo. We must fear the worst, shields up as well, you too this time Princess Sherry.”

Shields, again. What could it be this time? Ferris started to feel that all too familiar feeling of fright fiercely grip his spine.

“Yes Sir Blaze,” answered Sherry as she placed her quiver and her bow beneath her.

“I’m not imagining anything for you this time Ferret, you have to believe on your own.”

Ferris was too busy fixated on the fast approaching V formation above to heed Ryan’s warning. He could now make out the individual wings, bodies and beaks of the intruding flock. Apart from their annoying shrieks, the birds looked harmless enough, they didn't even seem to be that big. *Sir Blaze was probably being too overly cautious.* Ferris let out a quick sigh of relief as the birds swooped upwards.

"Whoooooooosh"

It was the proverbial calm before the storm.

"Incoming!" screamed the dragon knight. "Shields up!"

Shields?

Too late. The birds were back, darting downwards beak first towards the travelers. Midway between the ground and the cloud-line, Ferris noticed how the birds flapped open their wings in synchrony while simultaneously pooping out a blackish brown soil like substance from their bottoms. Ferris covered his face with his arms and was thankfully shielded by Sir Blazes left wing.

The foul brown colloid effortlessly melted its way through both Sir Blazes wings and the shields of the brother and sister Rogers. Ferris once again could barely believe his own two eyes, let alone all four. His ears though, were fully alert, as he recognized the sound the dark ooze made as it snaked its way through shield and dragon wing.

Pop Rocks!

"Take cover! They're circling back," warned Blaze as he guided his three companions to a nearby cleft in the gorge.

"What in Super Duper Land are those bedeviled things?" yelled Ryan.

"Stampheely Rakes, Major Commando. I'm usually too high in the sky to notice them. Apparently they feed on the darkest of chocolate barks, which is why their number two is so acidic."

Deadly dookies. This was supposed to be a walk in the park. Mallow Sparrows and Pompous Penguins. No one said anything about birds laying a deuce that could melt your face away.

"So what do we do now, shall I just shoot them down with my arrow?" volunteered Sherry.

"No your grace. It's too dangerous. We must find a way to distract them first."

"Hmmmm, I think I've got it. I used to distract my terrible sister all the time with this rattle my dad got her. Do you think that would work?" added Ryan.

"Perhaps." said Blaze

A rattle?

"What, is that the best you could come up with cousin?" screamed Ferris. His blood was boiling now, his fear turning into both anger and despair. "I think I've just about had it Ryan with all your hair-brained ideas." Ferris then shoved his cousin right in the chest as he fell victim to the most common outlet for fear during battle - rage.

"Well, I'm sick of you too," Ryan said as he shoved back.

"Eyaaaaw!"

No sooner than Ryan had shoved Ferris out, did two of the Stampheely Rakes swooped down and scooped up the furiously fearful knight of Bebounty. The air was filled with Ferris' screams.

****

Ferris felt the air get cooler as he was carried higher and higher by the two rakes. He immediately noticed how sharp and solid their beaks were and was surprised that they hadn't pierced his shoulders through his shirt.

Mum would kill me if I ruined my beach shirt, but I first need to survive this whole ordeal. Think silly Ferret, think. What would Sir Blaze do? Who would a true knight believe?

As Ferris hovered above in *beak-ween* the rakes. Major Commando Mega Jumbo prepared to administer his plan. The sound of his golden megaphone squeaking to life was deafening. The flyig knight of Bebounty could hear it even from all the way up.

"Now listen here you silly Stampheely squatters! Leave my cousin alone or my friend Blaze here will burn you to a crisp. I could do me with some cluckin' good chicken sandwiches."

"Yeah, you bird brains better drop him, or else?" added Sherry.

No you dodos. Not from up here!

Too late. The birds acquiesced and Ferris found himself plunging down to Earth for his hat trick of falls. Even though he was free falling, Ferris felt fortunate to be free of the rakes. Fortunately, or unfortunately, depending on which way you want to slice it, the falling knight of Bebounty found himself at the mercy of two lower flying rakes when he instinctively grabbed each with one of his hands. He was a giant cross in motion, dangling spread eagle in midair.

"Outstanding," remarked Sir Blaze.

And standing out is exactly what Ferris found himself doing next. Unbeknownst to him, two different (even lower flying) rakes found their way underneath him and somehow got tied up in the fallen laces of his sneakers. Yes, Ferris now had rake skates and was skating across the sky. In an attempt to balance himself, the suspended knight of Bebounty had rammed the two fistful of birds together, causing a domino effect with the rest of the flying V.

Sherry quickly capitalized on the confusion and simply shot down each of the tail spinning Stampheelys. The princess was actually such a good shot, that when Ferris was only but a few feet off the ground, she plucked two arrows from his quiver and fired both right underneath the fluttering knight of Bebounty's sneakers, skewering the two Stampheelys in one miraculous shot and forcing Ferris to fall flat face into the mud below.

Ferris was so overcome by delight to be back on 'solid' ground, that he hugged the mud as tightly as he could. Another sticky adventure coming to a close, only this time,

Ferris felt a different sort of feeling. It was more of a spark, slowing igniting amongst the embers of exhilaration that ensconced his heart earlier. Did he actually just enjoy his plight of a flight?

“Bravo Sir Ferris, another outstanding display of knighthood if I ever did see one. Meiyo to you!”

“Mei-who?” asked Ryan. The Major Commando was obviously overrun with jealousy. “He just kept on falling Sir Blaze?”

“Of course Major Ryan, all the great knights make even the most dangerous of feats look easy. They do it with honor and they do it because they enjoy it, hence the Eagle, which symbolizes the important virtue of knighthood - Meiyo or Honor. The Eagle is always smiling, even when flying, or as some might say falling, through the most precarious of situations. But I don’t have to tell you that do I Sir Ferris the Furious! Har Har!”

Ferris newfound feeling of fun quickly morphed into that giant bolus of guilt he had choked on earlier. He noticed a pattern developing and wondered how long he could keep up his charade. The deceitful knight of Bebounty was quick to hide his inner shame.

Chapter 13 - Rei

Ferris' feet were singing. Fatigue had set in throughout his body, but his feet were ringing in pain as he folded the bunny ears and laced up his sneakers. He noticed that his socks were actually quite wet and also terribly smelly. He must have sweated buckets these past few hours. Never a dull moment in Super Duper Land.

The tired travelers had now made their way out of the gorge and were about to make their way towards a field of tall swaying sugar canes covered with sweet caramelized popcorn, to gorge themselves, when Ferris again, was the first to notice something amiss.

"Wait a sec you guys, look over there, someone or something is lying flat down on their face."

"By Jove you are right Sir Ferris, it's a crone," blurted out Blaze confidently. "What's a poor old woman like her doing all the way out here."

Upon closer inspection, Ferris noticed that the fallen woman was old, but also cat like in a way. Her hair and whiskers were as white as the milk river Ryan had fallen into earlier this wacky day. The crone had a grimacing countenance about her that made Ferris both sneerful and fearful.

"We have to help her," pleaded Ferris. This poor old woman reminded him of his dear Boumi. He wondered if he would ever see her or his uncles, aunties and parents ever again.

“I think she’s dead,” exclaimed Sherry. “She’s not moving.”

“Lots of things don’t move but are still alive stupid sister. Trees for example and coral in the sea.”

“Duhhhh doofus, but they at least sway. She’s just...laying there.”

“With all due respect your grace, Major Commando Mega Jumbo is right. This crone seems to yet live. We must find out what ails her, any ideas Sir Ferris?”

Ferris furrowed his forehead feigning deep thought. He had no idea why this seemingly poor old woman was collapsed in front of a sweet popcorn sugarcane field. He did however notice through a small gape in her mouth that her tongue was as white as her hair and whiskers. You see, both Ferris’ parents were nerdy old doctors and they would usually discuss their medical cases during dinner time. Ferris remembered how one of his mum’s patients collapsed right in front of her in the hallway of the hospital. He remembered his mother saying something about a white tongue, but he couldn’t remember what it was. He did remember however, that his mother asked the nurses to bring the patient some orange juice and that that had made the patient feel much better and eventually regain consciousness. With no milk river in sight, Ferris hypothesized that this old cat lady was suffering from the same disease as his mother's patient.

But did they even have diseases in Super Duper Land?

“Does anyone have any orange juice?” he asked trepidatiously.

“Hmmmm...would nectar of the mango suffice?” asked Sir Blaze.

“I guess so, they’re both are yellow and taste sweet. Oranges are a bit sourer though.”

“And you say that this fruity elixir will cure this old crone of whatever spell she is under?”

“I think so”

“You *think* so?” clarified the dragon knight.

“No, no, I believe it to be so,” said Sir Ferris the Confident.

“Very well, Princess Sherry, over there yonder is a Mango Tango Tree, use your arrows to clip down the choicest morsels. It will also allow you to practice your aim. I noticed it was a bit off during the Stampheely raid.”

“With pleasure Sir Blaze.” Sherry was up to the challenge and quickly clipped down three of the highest mangoes.

“Now Major Commando Mega Jumbo, would you be so kind so as to retrieve those fallen tango mangos? I’m afraid the previous two battles have dwindled my energy and I must need to rest.”

“Of course Sir Blaze, it would be my Meiyo. That means honor...Sir Feeeeesiiii.” Ferris was all too familiar with Ryan’s tone. He knew his cousin was acting up, but chose not to shove him this time, either physically or verbally.

As Ryan scuttled to the tango tree, Sir Blaze wrapped his giant right arm around his fellow knight and whispered in his ear.

“Sir Ferris, I must confess that I am aware of your secret.”

“What, really, ummm, brave Sir Blaze, I can explain.”
“No, no explanation is needed my friend. Instead it is I who owe you the apology.”

Huh?

“Why should you apologize to him?” asked Sherry.

“Because your grace, Ferris is more noble as a knight than I could ever be. You see, I had lost my stripes for insulting my great foe, the Griffin, after one of our legendary aerial combat spars. In a word, I failed to exhibit Rei.”

“I suppose you're going to tell us what Rei means? Or do you prefer Sir Ferris to explain?” added Sherry with acidity.

“Sir Ferris is welcome to, as a true knight, he always exhibited this all important virtue of knighthood - Respect, or as us knights call it…”

“Rei,” blurted out Ferris softly. “Oppps, excuse me Sir Blaze, did not mean to steal your thunder.”

“By all means Sir Ferris. You see my dear Princess Sherry; he is polite too. He has been sparing us the showing off that many would-be knights exhibit to their comrades after the dust of battle has settled. He is as polite as the

Peacock, the sacred sigil of the virtue of Rei, commanding respect and never fanning out his beauty unless appropriate. He is respectful of Major Commando Mega Jumbo, even though, and please forgive me for saying this about your cousin Sir Ferris, even though he sometimes does not deserve your respect."

Ferris was strangely enjoying this. The lump in his throat somehow got smaller and he felt a great weight lifted off of his shoulders.

"No offense taken Sir Blaze, so you lost your stripes because you were not respectful in defeat?"

"Quite the contrary Sir Ferris. I did not exhibit Rei in victory, not defeat. Even now my blood boils at the thought of someone even assuming that that dastardly griffin could ever hope to defeat me. My pride is the reason why the Council of Elders stripped me of my stripes. That and other reasons. But come now, our comrade has returned with the fallen bounty and we must turn our attention back to the crone. Major Commando Ryan, commence the squeezing of the mangoes into the mouth of the old woman."

As Ryan squeezed the tangy nectar into the small space left open by the old crone, something very strange happened. The old woman's skin became smoother and darker, similar to the color of the popcorn fields afoot. Her eyes too slowly opened and her mane and whiskers grew thicker and darker still. She then let out a mighty growl. *ROOOOOOOOOOAR!*

Chapter 14 - Gi

Ferris immediately fell back.

The old lady's roar was as deafening as it was scary, only she wasn't as old anymore as she first seemed. The sugary sweet mango tango elixir had somehow revved the old lady back into a younger, more predatory state. Ferris was now far less concerned with her own well-being and instead was more concerned with his own. So much for the virtue of Rei.

Ryan and Sherry were both huddled behind Blaze, who was quick drew his giant shield and club. The lioness was much smaller than either of Sir Blaze's weapons, but much larger than Ferris, Ryan and Sherry. Her fur and mane were now richly caramel colored, with the mane much darker than the rest of the body. The lioness stood up on all four of her legs and proceeded to rip to shreds the old lady clothes off of her body. Ferris was terrified by the site. It was perhaps the most unexpected display of brutality he had yet to see with his own four eyes. The threat of impending doom he had felt earlier in the day, of both the Twydra and the Stampheely birds, rose once again within. It rose gradually like a menacing staccato of impending peril. This lioness, however, was a forte of ferocity bursting to life.

"Sir Ferris, arm yourself," instructed the dragon knight with great haste, "and fall into position."

Ferris scrambled his way up and miraculously found the Yu to believe in a golden suit of armor, helmet and all. No sooner had he gift wrapped his body in gold, did the lioness pounce on him, crashing our four eyed hero down to the floor. Her claws were of such immense power that they easily left scratch marks in the aureus armor.

Ferris was too scared to scream. The lioness was now gnawing at this helmet. Her sharp saber teeth gnashing into the visor and crest of the helmet. The petrified knight of Bebounty remained dumbstruck. It was terrifying site that left him tongue tied.

"Knights of Adailiya! Your cousin has the Gi of a Bear, look at how still he is, yet another great stratagem," commended the bulldog faced dragon. "Princess Sherry, on my mark, unleash your arrows of truth."

"I suppose Gi is the virtue of knighthood that involves standing still? Reminds me of Yin Yoga," bickered Ryan.

"I do not know this Yin Yoga you speak of, but Gi is our code of Integrity, symbolized by the Bear Major Commando. The bear stands tall in the face of adversity. He is still during the hunt and is one of the most centered beings in all of creation."

"Ready to loose on your command Sir Blaze."

"Excellent, fire at will your grace."

The arrows ricocheted off the lioness' hide almost as quickly as they left Sherry's bow. It seemed that the lioness' fur was harder than the hardest caramel candy, you know, the one that breaks your teeth if you try to bite into it as opposed to letting it slowly melt in your mouth.

Defeated by the petrous fur of the lioness, Blaze decided to bang his colossal club against his mammoth of a shield. The noise was as deafening as the lioness' earlier growls.

"Over here you dastardly demoness, over here," yelled Sir Blaze.

The lioness, seeing as Sir Ferris was so dutifully covered by his armor, turned her attention towards the boisterous dragon knight. Licking her lips, the lioness assumed a crouching approach, crawling softly towards Sir Blaze. It was a soundless, almost sensual, cantabile-like approach that rapidly escalated once again into a fierce forte once the lioness bolted towards Blaze.

She jumped in the air with all her might, only to land spread eagle on the dragon's shield, her body in the shaped on a giant X, a giant target.

"Now Major Commando, cast your axe into the beast's back."

Ryan, finally excited to be back in the game, threw his axe with all his might at the arched out feline. Ryan's disappointment rung louder than the sound the axe made when it limply bounced off of the back of the lioness.

Sir Blaze, needing time to think, threw away his shield like a giant discus, deep into the caramel corn field.

Great, thought Ferris, *now we can't even see our death coming towards us.* He had recovered his stance and joined his two cousins and fellow knight in a small semi-circle facing the cultivated sea of swaying stalks. Ferris wished that breeze would cease to blow, so that the movements of their impending doom would be easier to catch. The lioness' growls also seemed to come from everywhere, Ferris knew that he needed a bird's-eye view, but there were no tall trees close by and Sir Blaze's wings were probably still out of commission.

ROAAAAAAR.

The lioness leapt out of her camouflaged caramel corn field and landed on Ferris' poor unsuspecting female cousin, Sherry. Thankfully, her Sherryness had the sense to use her bow as a makeshift bulwark, pressing it against the lioness neck and staving her razor bites away.

"Nooooo!"

Ferris found a hidden strength as he tumbled towards his cousin. Remember that the timid knight of Bebounty was covered from head-to-toe in a heavy gold armored suit. Although his mechanical gait made it look as if he was moving in slow motion, his trip had quite the opposite feeling.

Ferris found himself falling face first into the dirt once again, in fast forward motion. Miraculously, his angle of descent caught the Super Duper sunlight at a blinding angel, casting a scorching ray from the helm of his helmet into the eyes of the rabid lioness, blinding her instantly.

The confused cat winced away from the fallen princess as it tried to shake the sun out of its eyes.

"Why excellent plan Sir Ferris, we all know that big cats are nocturnal and therefore hate the sunlight. Major

Commando, follow Sir Ferris' lead and reflect the sunlight off of your armor and into the eyes of that barbaric she devil!"

Ryan was at the ready and confidently angled his own red metallic armor, catching the rays of sun on his chest and bouncing them towards the confused cat. The light had more than a menacing effect on the lioness. She then started to spring sideways in pain, trying her best to avoid the light, which was now coming from all four corners of the square circle made up by the three Dum Dums and Sir Blaze. Light on light until the lioness could take it no more, and she was forced to claw away at her own eyes. You see, while her caramel fur was impervious to arrows and axes, it was not impervious to lioness' own claws, which dealt the final fatal blow to the crazed cat.

"Wow, that was super intense," whispered Ryan. He was right. The deadly speed and prowess of the now motionless feline was the most harrowing experience our heroes had yet to face.

"Truly spoken Major Commando, we would have all been minced meat had it not been for the Gi and Yuuki or Sir Ferris. I believe you have grown tired of my salutes fellow knight, but I am bound by the eagle-code of Meiyo to salute you once again."

As with every salute before, Ferris could feel the lump in his neck grow larger and larger. It was now dragon sized.

Chapter 15 - Chu

Having traversed through the treacherous gorge of the Stampheely birds and having carefully crossed the caramel colored popcorn fields of the fallen lioness, our heroes bent their steps towards the foot of a large mountain made of many giant marble like protrusions.

“Jawbreaker Mountain.” Announced Sir Blaze. “I must say that this is the first time I will have to climb it on foot.”

“You mean we all have to climb that?” squalled Sherry.

“Yes your grace, the gates to Annonovoburg are yonder past the Jawbreaker. It pains me to say that my wings are not yet ship shape if you would.”

Ship shape. Ferris allowed himself to day dream back to his days of staring out his bedroom window in Kay City, where he would count the number of boats on a postcard perfect day. The knot in his throat had subsided somewhat, but the constant gruesome glares he was getting from his cousin Ryan prevented the lump from sinking all the way down. Ryan would also roll his eyes frequently at the apprehensive knight of Bebounty, causing his stomach to also roll over with shame.
“After you Sir Blaze,” blurted out Commando Mega Jumbo, his eyes still fixated on Ferris. “Lead the way.”

As our heroes ascended the flattened base of the mountain, Ferris was focused on the multitude of differenced colored, yet perfectly round spheres jutting out from underneath the path. He plucked one and licked it pensively before popping it into his mouth.

CRUUUUUUUNCH!

No wonder they call it Jawbreaker Mountain.

As the first knight of Bebounty carefully crushed the giant gumball in between his jaws, trying his best to stop it from getting caught in between his gum line exposed by his missing two front teeth, Ferris was again the first to witness a giant cross blocking the setting Super Duper Land sun. Before he had a chance to point out the anomaly above, he felt familiar beads of sweat drip down his spine, a peristalsis of impending doom rendered him mute once again.

"Woah, watch out guys, is it a giant Stampheely? Or maybe it's your old foe the Griffin?" screamed Ryan.

"No!" hushed Sir Blaze. "There can only be one creature big enough to block out the sun. It is the Rukh."
"A flying rock?" inquired her Sherryness.

"Not rock princess. Rukh," corrected Blaze using a rich guttural sound that resonated loudly out from his long dragon neck.

"It's from the One Thousand and One Nights," added Ferris. "Buncle Murphy read it to us one night remember? The Rukh is a giant bird with giant claws big enough to carry an elephant and a beak big enough to eat an entire man in one bite. You are not too far off Sherry, they call it...a flying mountain."

"Correct Sir Ferris. Now we must take cover. The Rukh comes back during the twilight to feed its young. Best not to have it confuse us with their supper," warned the dragon knight.

Our heroes continued to creep up the mountain side, which grew progressively steeper and steeper until they could no longer climb anymore by walking. Instead, the travelers had to now rely on their arms and upper body strength. Ferris enjoyed this part. He was a master climber and smirked at the sight of Sherry clinging tightly onto Blazes throat. Ferris also enjoyed the fact that he was clearly beating Ryan up the mountainscape. Major Commando Mega Jumbo was no match for the spider knight of Bebounty.

Having reached the summit first, Ferris decided to reward himself by sniffing the cool mountain air. He enjoying the way his sneakers were leaving soft footprints on the powdery surface which was coarsely divided by strange weed like extensions that looked like long jagged scars. Strangely enough, the snow didn't feel cold, but Ferris was convinced that it might taste sweet, as everything seemed to taste sweet in Super Duper Land, only when the bitter danger of death no longer loomed. Surely enough, the chalky cover of Mt. Jawbreaker's summit was consumed by none other than powdered sugar, pancake perfect powder. The vines were tough and had both the texture and the taste of sour string candy. Ferris looked back and noticed the faint glow of Bubble Gum City in the distance. They had traveled a great deal today and he wondered what lay in store for the rest of their journey. As the sun continued its dive towards Annonovoburg, Ferris' ears were filled with an eerie, freaky, chirping noise. As he inched closer towards the noise, the faint-hearted knight of Bebounty heard a wicked whirl that froze him solid. The sounds seemed to be seeping out from the ground below, rumbling from the deep inner core of the giant mountain.

“Why so glum chum?” whistled Ryan as he hoisted himself, axe first of course, onto the summit of Mt. Jawbreaker.

“Shhhhhhh,” hissed Ferris. “Listen.”

The whirly chirpies gave both of our climbers the heebie jeebies.

“It’s coming from below,” presumed Ryan.

“What’s coming from below?” added Sherry as she slid her way down Sir Blaze’s neck like a fireman sliding down a pole.

“Shhhhhh, listen.” repeated Ferris

“Those must be the sounds of Rukh hatchling,” announced Sir Blaze.

“Only one way to be sure,” chuffed Ryan. “Sir Blaze, your knightly arm if you would be so kind.”

Sir Blaze immediately knew what the Major Commando wanted. He extended his right arm towards Ryan, who had just fixed his golden axe on the back of his armored suit, which had been reduced to a simple breast and back plate so as to not to burden the Major Commando on his climb up.

“On your mark,” yelled Ryan as he slammed down the visor of his helmet.

"Proceed," commanded the dragon knight.

It was a swift, seamless motion, unlike anything Ferris had ever seen. With one fell swoop, Ryan grabbed onto the chocolatey palm of their dragon friend with both hands and quickly hoisted himself up only to quickly arch his head back down by pushing his feet against the bottom part of Sir Blaze's extended forearm and wrist. Ryan looked like a red metallic vampire bat, hanging upside down, as Sir Blaze slowly lowered his arm past the mountain's edge.

A real spider knight! Thought Ferris, or Spider Major Commando to be more accurate. The now jealous knight of Bebounty heard the shrills of the Rukh's young frantically increase, higher and higher their chilling chirps got louder and louder until suddenly…

SLICE! SLICE! SLICE!

...there were no more sounds rising from beneath the ground. The only thing coming up from the Mountain's core was his cousin Ryan, who was rigged back up by Sir Blaze and covered in a reddish slime and black feathers. Ferris was sure that he also caught a waft of vanilla emanating from the hanging Commando.

"What...what have you done!" gasped Ferris

"Nothing," replied Ryan as he regained his footing on the mountain top. "They were so disgusting, they tried to attack me! I was just defending myself."

"They were children!"

"Demon birds! Plus they were making way too much noise, they would have alerted their mother, and that would have been the end of us!"

"No, it's quite the opposite actually. It is their silence that is now deafening...look!" yelled Ferris as he pointed towards the setting Super Duper sun.

Surely enough, the benevolent knight of Bebounty was right. The large Rukh had somehow noticed the lack of chirping coming from the nest near the pinnacle of the mountain. She was now heading towards our heroes at full speed. Ferris could feel his jaw drop in awe at the sheer size of the winged monstrosity.

What happens when a flying mountain crashes into another mountain? Ferris thought as he imagined the worst of what was yet to come.

"We must make haste," commanded the dragonknight. "I believe my wings have recovered enough to at least glide down. Hurry, climb up onto my back at once."

You didn't have to ask Ferris twice. In fact, he was ready to jump off the mountain himself. Without a moment's hesitation, the whitewashed knight of Bebounty jumped onto Sir Blaze's back and was quick to extend his arm to Sherry who joined at about the same time as Ryan, who flung himself right in front of Ferris.

"Wait!" cried Sherry. "Where's Hungry Bunny?"

"Who?" asked the chocolate dragon?

“It’s her uni-rabbit!” yelled Ferris. “Over there!”

In her haste, her Sherryness had forgotten to pick up her stuffed doll. Ferris’ quickly calculated that they would never be able to glide down in time if Sir Blaze had to trumble all the way back.

“Sir Blaze, go on without me!”

“But Sir Ferris, we can not…”

“Just go! I have a plan, trust in me.”

The flustered dragon acknowledged his fellow knight’s command with a begrudgingly somber node of the head. Ferris could feel the ground shake once again as Sir Blaze bounced off Mt. Jawbreaker and briskly plunged to the depths below. He also noticed the Rukh’s shadow now menacingly covering the summit. He had no time to waste, he reached down and tore one of the large red root-like extensions and fashioned it into a formidable rope. Ferris quickly fastened himself using one end before successfully looping the other end around a giant gumball boulder as a makeshift licorice lasso. All instinct, he promptly grabbed Hungry Bunny and quickly swerved off of the mountain’s edge as the gargantuan flying beast crashed its Pac-Man sized beak into the rope’s purchase point, severing the lariat in two and snapping the falling knight of BeBountry right into the nest below.

It was darker than Ferris could have imagined, but then again, the Rukh was either easily blocking the remaining light of the setting sun, or the sun itself had finally set on this most hazardous of days. The black and blue knight of Bebounty could feel his muscles ache as the supposedly well-hidden nest shook from the above movements of the Rukh. The creature was now screeching angrily above and Ferris knew that it would soon clumber around to check in on its hatchlings.

Instinctively, Ferris began to gather the passel of feathers left over from Ryan's slicing spree. He stuck them onto every part of his and Hungry Bunny's body using the sticky vanilla smelling substance that covered the Rukh's crypt-like roost.

A deadly smell of vanilla filled the air as the Rukh peered, beak first, below the mountain's edge. Ferris decided that his only hope was the closely mimic the sounds of the recently departed baby birds.

"Rrrrrr rhirp....Rrrrrrr rhihirp," the panicked knight of Bebounty tweeted hopefully as the Rukh's slowly shifted its face sideways, revealing a menacing giant red eye. Ferris could see his reddish reflection in the fiery eye and knew that he had to now truly earn his Virtue of Yu. He closed his own eyes and kicked a sizeable gum ball right into the bird's black iris.

The Rukh's squawked in pain, it's harsh, piercing cry shook both the nest and the lair around it so vociferously that Ferris found himself on a treacherous toboggan ride down the bumpy mountain slope of Mt. Jawbreaker. The nest twisted and twirled as Ferris hurled out whatever candy remained in his stomach.

The Rukh, having somewhat recovered from the knightly scuff kick, decided to focus its rage on the descending baby butcher that was skidding down the mountainscape in pinball machine fashion. Ferris could feel the gusts of wind from the Rukh's wings break against his newfangled nest sled. The sheer force of the flapping easily tore off the small twigs from the side of the twirling nest and forced the limp bodies of its lifeless young overboard. These strong squalls were followed by more deafening squawks as the flying leviathan levitated its way closer and closer to the fully feathered Ferris. Despite the instability and great speed of his descent, Ferris could readily see his party of travelers waiting for him by the mouth of a large tunnel that seemed to go through the malicious massif at the foot of the mountain.

****

"Come on Sir Ferris," willed Sir Blaze openly. "Major Commando, help me fell this tree."
"Yes sir!" said Ryan, as he busily hacked away at the base of a large chocotree that was part of the tree line that separated the foot of Mt. Jawbreaker from a welcomed tunnel.

"And this one as well," ordered the dragonknight as he pushed the first tree down with all his wyverian might.

Ryan rapidly shifted his stance and chopped down the second chocotree with ease, for the second tree was a white chocotree and they were known to be more fragile than the darker variety.

"Excellent, now grab the tip of the brown tree and on my command, heave it towards me."

"With pleasure Sir Blaze"

"Princess, please roll that rock towards me as well."

“You got it Blaze.”

“Thank you,” concluded the dragon as he gyrated his center of mass to stack all his might into his his tail which he then flicked towards the white chocotree, felling it easily with one fell swoop. He then hastily laid both trunks in a V-like position, with the pointy end of the V resting on the rock Sherry had recently rolled over. The V was pointing towards Sir Ferris and the falling nest.

“Yes! I can see it now. Ferret is going to love the final loop,” chuckled the Major Commando.

He was wrong. So wrong.

Ferris felt his heart stop as the rotating nest crashed into the wooden V ramp. It was a similar sensation that Ferris had once felt at the local skate park back in Kay City, except that this time there was a crazed behemoth of a bird closing in on him. The crash caused the remains of the Rukh’s roost to capsize and catapult Ferris head first towards the tunnel. Thankfully, our airborne knight of Bebounty had a death grip on Hungry Bunny, who followed Ferris Four Eyes right into the outstretched arms of the dragonknight.

“Gotcha!” exclaimed Sir Blaze. “Now follow me!” he added as he charged his way deep into a mountainous passageway that separated Mt. Jawbreaker from the cliff rock borders of Annonovoburg.

“Right behind you,” yelled Ryan.
“Oh my gosh Sir Ferris, thank you for saving Hungry Bunny! You’re my hero!” added Sherry as they both followed the bulldog faced dragon into the burrowed

entrance. Our heroes were now safely shielded from the praying beak of the Rukh, which followed them half way into the tunnel, screeching menacingly (and no doubt fully frustrated) at having failed to avenge the death of its offspring.

But Ferris never heard those shrills and experiences none of the flying thrills. His vomit filled pole vault through the air had rendered him blissfully unconscious mid-way into Sir Blaze's arms.

Emerging from the dark depths of the massif tunnel, our heroes basked in the glow of a rising full moon. It's intense light helped ease Sir Ferris back into the land of the waking.

"Where...where are we?" Asked the half-awake knight of Bebounty as he was hammocked tightly in the arms of Sir Blaze, with a full upwards viewpoint of the dragon's protruding chin.

"Resting are we Sir Ferris? We are almost at the gates of Annonovoburg and Castle De Annonovo is just there yonder. My my that was quite display of Chu!"

"Gesundheit!" squealed Sherry.

"Silly Sherry, he said Chu not Ah-chu!" corrected Major Commando Mega Jumbo.

"Quite right Major Commando, Chu or Chuugi is yet another virtue of knighthood displayed by our brave Sir Ferris on this dastardly day."

“I suppose you are going to tell us what it means now” humphed Sherry.

“If it please your grace.”

“Yes, it would please me very much,” snickered Her Sherryness.

“Very well, Chu or Chuugi is our knight speak for the all-important virtue of Loyalty. Like its symbol, the Wolf, a knight must always expose loyalty especially towards a fallen comrade, such as your Hungry Bunny. Indeed, it is most knightly, to always display compassion to the weakest of creatures. Wolves, as I am sure you both know, never hunt alone either, they form packs and look after one another. A knight must be as loyal as a wolf and must always lead by example. Bravo Sir Ferris, Bravo.”

“Awoooooooooooo,” howled Ryan. “I like being part of a wolf pack.”

“Awoooooooooooo,” howled Sherry. “So do I.”

“Awoooooooooooo,” howled Sir Blaze. “I have become the dragon wolf!”

Ferris remained quiet as the other three travelers howled wildly at the waxy full moon. His howling was an inner, more melancholic one.

Chapter 16 - Jin

The moon had fully risen over the Super Duper Landscape as our four heroes, O.K. five if we count Hungry Bunny, approached the towering gates that marked the official border of Annonovoburg. The gates were three times as tall as Sir Blaze and surrounded by a deep defensive moat that reflected the moonlight willingly, thus providing an awe inspiring halo effect around the entrance to the city.

“Right, make yourself presentable gentle knights and fair lady and prepare to present your passes to the sentinels,” directed Sir Blaze.

Flamingo guards noticed Ferris, their pink shields and spikes made him feel at ease.

“Uh oh,” exclaimed Ryan. “The passes, I…. I can’t remember where I put them.”

“You what?” yelled Ferris in disbelief. “How could you lose them? Especially after making such a fuss at the Mayor's office.”

“I...I don't know,” sniveled the Major Commando. “Sherry, do you have them?”

“Don’t look at me doofus. I have my own pass right here,” she said proudly as she flashed her papers in Ryan’s winced face.

“Perhaps we can explain our situation to the Baron of Jawbreaker Pass, he is known to be earnest and fair in greeting travelers from Dum Dum World.”

“Hey, who you calling Dum Dum.... ummmm.... you fireless mouth breather?” Countered the loud mouthed Mega Jumbo.

“My apologies if I have offended you Major Commando. For it was not my intent to do so. The Dum Dum world is simply what us Super Duper Lander’s call the world from whence you came.”

Fair Enough. Thought Ferris. It was certainly an accurate description of his cousin Ryan by his account.

“I know that, I’m sorry Blaze, I’m just angry that I lost our paperwork,” admitted the Major Commando.

“Tell us more about this Baron, Sir Blaze,” asked the inquisitive knight of Bebounty.

“Aye, I have never met him before, but they say that he is blue in complexion, with a flat face but an amiable nature. He is shrewd in judgement, yet joyful in demeanor.”

Sounds awfully familiar, Ferris thought as he glanced towards his cousin. But before the curious knight of Bebounty could ask another follow up question, he was interrupted by the groaning sound of a trumpet.

Babababdoooooooo.....Babababdoooooo!

“Who approaches my gates at such an hour?” inquired a nasal voice from high above the tower.

“It is I my lord, Sir Blaze of House Barras-Hargan and my three companions, Sir Ferris the Furious of House Bebounty, Major Commando Mega Jumbo and Princess Her Sherryness of House Razzmatazz. We seek safe passage to Castle Annonovoburg.”

“Very well, papers please!” yelled the voice.

“Here’s mine,” yelled the princess in her high pitched voice.

The shadowy figure emerged into the moonlit balcony overlooking the four travelers, who were arching their heads backwards from the foot of the draw-bridge.

“Ah yes,” spoke the voice as Ferris noticed a blue hoof like hand adjust a green monocle. He suspected that this was the blue Baron of Jawbreaker Pass that Sir Blaze was blathering on about. Ferris also figured out the source of his nostalgia, the flat face of the Baron was accentuated by a protruding and equally blue snout.

“Proceed your grace. Augy Tower is honored by your visit. Sentinels prepare guest rooms for the princess and her dragon knight,” commanded the pig-faced and pork-bodied Baron.

“Hey, what about us!” screamed Ryan.

“Present your papers and you shall pass too,” countered the Baron. “Otherwise these gates will remain locked to you.”

"That's a load of pi..." Thankfully Ryan was interrupted by his cool tempered cousin.

"My Lord. We have traveled great lengths and defeated many a notorious foe to be here. We simply seek some shelter for the night and we promise to be on our way before daybreak. I swear to you by the Virtues of Gi and Rei that we have simply misplaced our papers, most likely whilst saving a small village in your noble dominion from the deadly Twydra."
Silence. Ferris had expected quite a different outcome after such knightly discourse.

"Twydra you say," the silence was finally broken by the same loud nasal voice of the Baron.

"Step closer puny knight."

Ferris did as asked, casually motioning for Ryan to both calm down and stay back. The somber knight of Bebounty gingerly stepped onto the drawbridge. His steps were interrupted by the sound of a large thud in the darkness ahead.

The Baron was twice the height of Ferris but still much shorter than Size Blaze, when it came to sheer girth. Ferris imagined that both the Baron and the dragonknight probably weighed the same. He also wondered how the giant blue hog could support all his weight on his two small feet. He then wondered how thick the drawbridge must be to support the weight of the big blue Baron jumping from twenty feet high.

"So, you are the one that defeated the Twydra?" asked the sweaty Baron of Jawbreaker Pass.

“Indeed, it was us who defeated him. Using our Chuugi,” explained Ferris as he looked over his shoulder towards Sir Blaze and his two cousins.

“I see,” continued the Baron. “Then I am obliged to let you pass, but only on one condition.”

Ferris remained silent. He figured that his silence was both the best way to maintain his command of the situation and the best way to also avoid finding his foot in his own mouth.

“The Augy stables have been filthy for generations. If you easily defeated the Twydra as you so claim, then you should make short work of cleaning my stables as well?”

Stables? Don’t you mean sties?

“Very well. We accept the challenge,” announced Ferris proudly.

“Then you have my word as Baron Augy of House Hoggy and Custodian of the Gates to Annonovoburg that you shall pass once my stables are spick and span.”

****

“I wish you hadn’t fallen into that trap Sir Ferris,” scrunched Sir Blaze. “The Baron’s assignment seems to be both humiliating and impossible, since these foul smelling hogs both produce and wallow in enormous quantities of their own filth. These stables have never ever been cleaned, even since I was a hatchling, my father would tell me story after story about the hopeless mess that is the Augy Stables."

"No worries, Sir Blaze. How bad could it be really?" assured the confident knight of Bebounty as the four travelers had left the drawbridge and snaked their way round the banks of the moat towards the Augy Stables annexed to the tower bridge.
It was bad. Really bad. The stench was so foul and rancid that all four heroes had to quickly cover both their nostrils and their mouths and retreat back outside the pigsty-stables.

"You're on your own boys," Her Sherryness is sitting this one out.

The quick peak afforded to Ferris before the revolting humors overwhelmed his olfactory senses forced him to sink into a fatalistic sort of feeling. Both Ryan and Blaze, were too marred by bleakness. The stables were covered by mounds of brown manure that looked like giant molehills. The air was filled with flies who conspired to create a buzzing noise was almost as annoying as the toxic stench. It was the most disgustingly dirty, dusty, filthy, grimy, grotty, grubby, gungy, manky, messy, muddy, mucky, shabby, scummy, scungy, scuzzy, slummy, smeary, slimy, sticky, soiled, sooty, sordid, squalid scene Ferris had ever seen.

"I told you it was bad," shrugged Sir Blaze. I guess I should direct you good fellows back to Bubble Gum City?"

Ryan softly nodded in agreement. The mounds of dung that towered in every corner of the stable seemed like an insurmountable task for two Dum Dum boys and a dragon. Not for the persistent knight of Bebounty though.

"Gentlemen, or should I say gentleman and gentle dragon," began Ferris Four eyes confidently.

"We must come up with a solution, I think.... I think...."

"What is it Ferret, shall I ready my axe and make blue bacon out of the Baron?" asked the Major Commando menacingly.

Ferris flashed back to Baron Augy Hoggy bouncing up on the drawbridge. *Strange how he never fell right through into the moat. The moat! Of course.*

"No no no. We have an accord and it is my knightly duty to honor it. Meiyo remember."

"Right on Sir Ferris, Meiyo, our eagle-eyed code of honor," cheered Sir Blaze.

"Right, I think I have it. So Ryan, remember when we went mudding through the desert in Uncle Mark's truck?"

"Ya, so?" The Major Commando looked puzzled.

"So, how did we get the truck all cleaned up?"

"Ummmm.... wait....yes. We used a hose."

“Exactly! We let the water do the work for us.”

“So we make believe a hose?”

“No cousin, we move the moat.”

****

Sherry had finally settled into her bed. She had just given Hungry Bunny a hot bath to remove all those disgusting black Rukh feathers, she did miss the strong scent of vanilla. Her Sherryness decided that she was going to polish the rabbit’s horn on the balcony. Sherry strangely hoped that the horn would capture some of the shine off of the moonlight since she knew that both unicorns and uni-rabbits need their monthly moon light diet to keep their horn strong and firm.

Standing on the balcony overlooking the drawbridge and its surrounding moat, the pretty Princess of Razzmatazz noticed three shadows looming closer and closer to the water bank, one shadow was much larger than the other two.

“What are those three nincompoops doing now?”

Sherry could hear a steady hustle and bustle of murmuring, shoveling and the odd scolding. She also noticed the moonlit water slowly snaking its way away from the drawbridge following the largest of the shadows back towards the stables.

"Ah ha, he is using his tail, clever dragon," she whispered as she noticed the moonlight twinkle off of Hungry Bunny's horn.

****

It was just after daybreak when Baron Augy stormed into the stables.
"Ah ha! I told you...generations have tried and generations have fail..." The Baron's flat face was now gaping openly. The stables were sparkling. They looked brand spanking new. The Baron's black beady eyes fixated on the two citizens of the Dum Dum world snoring loudly on each of the broad shoulders of the dragonknight, who was also fast asleep.

"Eh Eheem"

The Baron looked to his lower left. It was the puny princess.

"I suggest you let them rest up for the rest of the morning. We'll be out of your hair by noon. I also suggest you fix me some breakfast. The Princess will have her pancakes well done, extra syrup please."

Her Sherryness could feel the disappointment brewing within the Baron's body. She stomped both her feet for emphasis: "At once my lord!"

"As you command your grace. Would you like any sprinkles or powder with that?"

“Why yes please. Sprinkles and syrup on the side though.”

****

Ferris could both feel and smell the moisture rising off of the paved marble that lined the stable floor. It reminded him of the brackish water park that he and Ryan had developed one hot summer day back in Kay City. It was sheer genius, climbing up the slide and setting the water hose to stream warm salty water down the slanted steel was an instant success. That is, until Ryan went down too fast and slid-slammed straight into Aunty Selma’s grove of palmlings.

“Rise and shine Sir Ferret,” greeted the way too chirpy Commando. “It’s almost noon sleepyhead.”

“The Major is right Sir Ferris, we best be on our way” said the stretching dragonknight.

Who knew dragon yoga was even a thing?

“Hiya cousin! Great job with the moat last night,” added Sherry.

“Thanks,” grouched the somnolent knight of Bebounty. “Did the Baron see the stables?”

“He did,” assured Sherry. “And boy was he ticked off.”
“Ya, Sherry says he was quite *swineful*! Ha Ha! Get it, it’s like spiteful but for….”

“Ya ya Ryan, I got it. So he is going to let us pass.”

“Indeed,” declared the dragon as he cracked both his back and neck noisily. “We are now only a farsang away from Castle Annonovo thanks to your *Jin*, Sir Ferris.”

“Wait, what's that?” enquired Ryan as he scarfed down a huge chocolate covered waffle morsel.

“What’s what?” replied Sir Blaze earnestly.

“A farsang is an old unit of measurement cousin, it's about an hour's walk back in olden times,” crowed the proud knight of Bebounty.

“Oh…OK, but I didn’t know you had a Jinn help us out last night. Sneaky Ferret!”

“Wait, I’m confused. You had genies help you out last night as well? You commanded the Jinn and all you asked for was to clean some gross stable!” Sherry was visibly upset.

Sir Blaze gave all three a consternated look. He was as confused as Sherry, but far more silent.

“No you nitwits. There are no genies in this realm,” scolded the bad tempered knight of Bebounty. “Are there Sir Blaze?”

“I know not of these genii you speak of. I was merely referring to the glorious but often neglected virtue of knighthood we call Jin. Like the ugly duckling that turns into a beautiful swan, this oft forgotten virtue is a marked by humility in the face of ridicule. Compassion must always prevail. Any important task, however small or in our case, however smelly, does warrant the full attention of a noble knight. No matter what the eventual outcome. A deep focus at the task at hand is a solemn pillar of knighthood."

"Well said Sir Blaze. Ferris has always been a big fan of Swan Lake," chuckled Ryan mischievously.

Ferris faked a yawn, pretending to be too languid to be concerned with the verbal jabs of the Major Commando. The unvarnished truth was that he was wide awake and ready to go and still very conflicted internally that he had never truly exhibited six out of the seven virtues of knighthood Sir Blaze had thus far explained throughout their treacherous journey.

Chapter 17 - Castle De Annonovo

"I bid thee farewell then Sir Ferris," pronounced the dragonknight. There was a hint of sorrow breaking across those seven words. "If you require any further assistance, just look to the sky ok?"

Ferris was flabbergasted by a sense of despair and remorse. *Could knights cry?*

"I hope you get your stripes back," chimed in Ryan.

"I know I will," assured the chocodragon. "You be weary of the Annonovosaurus now. I hear he can be quite boisterous when driving home his deals."

"Carry on Sir Blaze," said Sherry as she ran to hug their faithful companion. The dragonknight embraced the princess openly and peered over towards his fellow knight.

Ferris felt the weight of the Sir Blaze's piercing gaze. He decided that the best way to hide his own tears was to quickly cough away any chance of them building up and instead extend his right hand. The bulldog jawed dragon managed a polite smile as he extended the smallest of his four fingers in response.

"I salute thee, brave dragonknight," exclaimed Ferris as he did he best to mimic the Super Duper salute. He was soon joined by both his cousins as Sir Blaze reciprocated the salute and slowly began his march away from Annonovoburg. The dragonknight flapped open his wings and began flapping them vociferously, taking flight almost instantly, as gusts of wind blew away the tears drooping down Ferris eyelids.

****

Even from a far off distance, the castle was stupendous. It jutted out like a giant jagged tooth. Ferris had never seen anything like it. It was both simple and breathtaking at the same time. The minimalist trapezoid outline was surrounded by nine spiraling towers that reminded Ferris of the churros he loved to devour during the Kay City Fall Fair. There was more geometry to behold at Castle De Annonovo, for the main body of the castle was covered in an interesting interlocking confabulation of circular and hexagonal patterns that seemed to go on forever. Keeping with the county fair-theme, Ferris imagined that the large trapezoid was actually a massive funnel cake. He loved those too, probably even more so than the churros.

"Wow," exhaled Ryan. "It's huge!"

"Shall we?" ushered Sherry. "We came all this way."

"Right," blurted the reluctant knight of Bebounty. "But I am still unsure why we are here in the first place. Who is this Annonovosaurus and why is he important to me?"

"Don't you worry about that cousin," assured the Major Commando. "You just let me handle the *neghostiations*."

"You mean negotiations."

"Yes, the neghostiations. Spooky stuff isn't it."

Ferris shook his head in dismay as he followed Ryan towards the grand globulus gates of the castle, both Sherry and Hungry Bunny were a close step and a tug behind.

****

The gates were guarded by giant armored Ostriches. *More bird brained sentinels*. Ferris didn't like the way their eyebrows greeted him, but he had begrudgingly decided to blindly follow Ryan's lead . He knew that they had to stay focused on the task at hand. Ferris was actually quite curious to finally meet Mr. Annonovosaurus. It felt ages ago when both he and Ryan blew their way through the beach house living room and into this weird and wacky world of Super Duper Land.

"Hey there stretch, hello *beakiful*," started Ryan, admittedly not the best start to any conversation. The greeting prompted Ferris to remember the Rukh and how they had all escaped it's beak of death. This was indeed nothing compared to a pair of overweight ostriches with spears. Besides, ostriches had lost their ability to fly eons ago.

"Who goes there?" inquired one of the sentinels.

"It is I, Major Commando Mega Jumbo and my two traveling companions, Sir Ferris the Furious of House Bebounty and my good sister, Princess Her Sherryness of House Razzmatazz. Make way, for we have urgent business with your master."

"They seem regal enough," whispered the other goosier looking guard. "I vote they pass...Todd."

"Very well! You and your party may proceed Major Commando. Welcome to Castle De Annonovo!" Announced the Todd.

The magnificent and bulbous beige gate of Castle De Annonovo began to rise, inviting the three travelers to walk in, and revealing an interior decor that was just as stupendous as the outside of the castle. Passing through the gatehouse, Ferris marveled at the vast expanse of the castle's main bailey with its pristine, manicured lawns that were peppered with purple and pink flowers. The pathway then led towards a magnificent fore building, which protruded formidably out of the center of the large trapezoid which Ferris had noticed earlier from a distance. The top of the fore building was decorated with different colored flags and statues. The attentive knight of Bebounty made out a Black Bear on a Green Field, a silver Eagle spread eagle on a light blue escutcheon and a Pink Swan arched over a half green half blue cartouche. There were a few other statues and flags that he could not make out due to lack of wind and due to the fact that the Super Duper sun was rising once again.
Through the fore building they entered and were greeted by a long line of ostrich guards on either side of the pathway. There must have been at least one thousand of them standing erect in attention on each side, as far as Ferris four eyes could see.

"Now that's a farsang," cried Ryan.

"It's not that far!" corrected Sherry. "You can see the end dummy."

Sherry was correct. The distance was far flung from a farsang, but it did take Ferris and his two cousins almost fifteen full minutes to reach the end of the antechamber where another gigantic well carved beige door greeted them by drawing up ever so slowly, teasing them with every upwards pull. The pathway spilled into the largest room Ferris had ever seen with ceilings almost as high as Mt Jawbreaker.

It's the Throne Room.

Only there was no throne. The great hall was crowned by a domed azure roof glittered with the luster of what seemed to be hundreds of thousands of emeralds. The dome itself was supported by a network of 24 different windows adorned with bejeweled lattices made up of a priceless prism of gems. A single coco blanco desk was planted in the middle of the chamber with nothing but a lonely lit oil lamp resting on it. The lamp was slightly slanted towards the left, a sinister omen if there ever was one. Ferris could hear the sounds of their footsteps echoing up and down the colossal chamber as the trio slowly tiptoed their way towards the center.

"Greetings specimens." The sound came from above, but Ferris could not see anyone speaking.

Miraculously, the ceiling and the upper part of the wall facing our heroes began to shift out, revealing a spiraling stairwell with a large orange orb emerging at the top.

"The name's Alberti R. Annonovo Rex," continued the voice. "Entrepreneur Extraordinaire."

As the orb moved closer, Ferris noticed that it has two feet but no arms. Maybe a head as well, but certainly no arms. The orb was also most certainly wearing what appeared to be a giant black top hat.

"It's a pleasure to meet thee almost as much as it is a pleasure to be me. As you can see, I am an Annonovosaurus Rex, the last of my kind I am afraid. Or should I say sorry? Yes, Sorry, that would work better, or would it make my opening line too much of an enjambment?"

Of course. A walking talking orange dinosaur. Hence the -saurus in Annonovosaurus. Ferris flashed back to a hot and humid day in Kay City where he decided to spend the afternoon beating the heat and reading his favorite book, the Encyclopedia, in bed. He remembered how the word dinosaur came from the verbal marriage of two Greek words - *denios* meaning terrible and *sauros* meaning lizard. At least Mr. Annonovosaurus' entrance thus far, was far from terrible.

"What an enjambment?" asked Sherry.

"Why an enjambment is a word that means that you're wending your way along a line of poetry or prose only to find yourself walking right out to the very end of the line, way out, and it's all going fine, and you're expecting the syntax to give you a polite tap on the shoulder to wait for a moment.... But instead the syntax pokes at you and says hustle it, pumpkin, keep walking, don't rest. So naturally, because you're stepping out into nothingness, you fall. You tumble forward, gaaaah, and you end up all discombobulated at the beginning of the next line."

Ferris noticed the confused looks taking command of his two cousins' faces. Alberti R. Annonovo the last Annonovosaurus was a speedy speaker. He also had two large black fuzzy things crawling down either side of his face which contrasted greatly with his own orange face.

“Salutations kind sir...we,” started Ryan

“No no no, I am not a knight, I am but a lowly Baron. An industrial tycoon. Thenceforth, you may call me Mr. Annonovo, or Mr. Rex or by my initials HRAR.”

Ferris focused his stare on the side of the dinosaur who called himself Alberti.

“Delightful aren’t they,” cooed the Baron of Annonovoburg. “Now if you would be so kind to stop staring at my dundrearies, I believe we have some pressing business to attend to my lovelies.”

Ferris began to feel a tad bit embarrassed to be caught staring. He wondered if he should ask a question to deflect the dinosaur's attention. “What does the R. stand for?” blurted out the bashful knight of Bebounty. Ferris thought he was using his inner voice and was surprised to see orangey reptile acquiesce, although the response was far more from cordial.

“ROAAAAAAAAAAAAAAAAAAAAAAAAAAARK!” roared Mr. Rex. “Alberti Roark Annonovo. Now that I have introduced myself, would you be so kind to state your own names and *purpospsi*?”

“Most certainly, I am Major Commando Mega Jumbo and this is Sir Ferris the Furious of House Bebounty and this enjambment is my loud sister, Princess Her Sherryness of House Razzmatazz. We have traveled far and wide to be here with you today. We would like to make you an offer you dare not refuse.”

"Ah yes, quite right. I have heard of your escapades my dear specimens. Welcome to Annonovoburg. Indeed, I am intrigued by your offer as much as I have been intrigued by your opening line. It is the art of the deal that I am most infatuated by."

Ferris felt as if he was watching the scene unfolding in front of him from above. It was a strange feeling, approaching deja vu but still very eerily unfamiliar, quite surreal.

"I understand that you are in the birthday business." Ryan's question was more of statement.

"Yes, among other things," replied the Annonovosaurus snidely.

"Cool, well we have some extra special birthdays we wish to barter for entrance into the Annonovodome."

"Excelente caliente!" With a clap of his two scrawny clawed hands, Mr. Annonovo summoned two ostriches to speedily sandwich him between two opposing mirrors. One of the guards handed the Baron a long black cane which sparkled lustrously at one end.

"There are only two ways to approach infinity in this life. Mathematics and standing in between two looking glasspsi."

It was Ryan this time who gave a confused look to both his sister and his cousin.

“I’m not quite sure I follow sir...I mean Mr. Annonovo Rex,” asked Ferris politely.

“It’s quite simple my lovely. All birthday selling specimens must sign a contract. A contract is an agreement, a written down hand shake if you will, but the buyer and the stealer, sorry, the seller. Contracts are lengthy and full of large technical words, terms and conditions, but the mustard is simple. The trade is that each Dum Dum citizen must perform one math problem for me on their first day in the Annonovodrome, followed by two problems on the second, and four on the third and so on and so forth. A simple doubling each day, for the rest of your days. An Annonovosaurus has bills to pay you know, the Annonovodrome does not run on fairy dust! What say you?”

“Wow, only two problems a day, that’s nothing. So in one week we do only 14 math problems. Piece of cake. Mrs. Doran gives us way more on Math Mondays.” Ryan was always way too enthusiastic for Ferris’ taste.
“Hold on just a second,” paused Ferris. Something did not sit right with the skeptical knight of Bebounty. “What kind of math problems are we talking about?” *And why does a dinosaur need a walking cane with a diamond on it?*

“Why, nothing you smart specimens can’t do in your sleep I’m sure. As you can tell already my lovelies, I love geometry, there may be some trigonometry and some basic algebra, nothing too fancy I assure you. It’s basically for the blockchain. It will all be stated clearly in the contract. Shall I have my assistant draw up the papers?”

“Where can I sign!” Ryan had his pen at the ready. Ferris wondered where in the tar heels his cousins had gotten a large fountain pen with a poofy purple plume on the end, but that right now was the least of his concerns.

"Excelente caliente. Oh Professori. Papers if you please!" Announced the Annonovosaurus.

Mr. Wilcox was a different type of orange that his entrepreneurial employer. It was a darker and dirtier orange. He was also furry, not scaly, with snow-white whiskers and big coke bottle bottom glasses perched on a short black snout.

"You bellowed Master Annonovo?"

A walking talking fox, naturally, but why on earth is he dressed like a scientist?

"Ah yes, Professori Wilcox, please assuage all concerns of these gentledums and have them directly sign the contract. Blue ink please. All three names as per the usual."

"Hello poppets, and what are your delicious super-duper names?"

Sherry brushed the boys aside and yelled: "I am Princess Her Sherryness, First of My Name, Rightful Hair to House Razzmatazz and these are my two subjects, my bungling brother Major Commado Mega Dumbo and my cousin, Sir Ferret Four Eyes of House Bebounty."

"Very well, pay attention right here kind sirs and gentlelady. On the first page you will notice a detailed description of our distributed ledger technology. Picture the kind of hyper-simplified scenario economics eggheads love; ten Dum Dums buy and sell various kinds of....ummmm....sweets from each other using old dirty metal coins or paper money. Ferris sells Ryan one of his sweeties for a coin, Sherry buys two of Bobby's sweets for three coins, and so on. When everybody's done buying and selling for the day, there's no question of how rich or poor they are: they can just count their coins or bills right?"

"Right!" yelled out Sherry. Ferris was glad someone else was paying attention. He glanced over at Ryan as well, who seemed miles away.
Mr. Wilcox continued, "Now, things get a bit more complicated if we introduce something called credit."

"You mean like the cards cut up by Auntie Vanessa?" blurter Sherry.

"Exactly," Professor Wilcox the Fox was on a roll. "So now imagine that your Aunt Vanessa owes Ferris a coin, and I owe you three, but we do not use any actual real coins. They are all computer coins, what we call digital currency."

"I thought dino currency would have had a better ring to it, but dino can means terrible you see," added the Annonovosaurus.

Dino means Terrible. Terrible Money, thought Ferris.

"Back to our credit scenario, you can easily see that any self-interested and sufficiently motivated sweet aficionado would take note of their transactions, which is a fancy word for buying and selling, in order to keep track of what they owe and what others owe them. But unless every party is perfectly honest and implausibly scrupulous, never forgetting to carry a 1 or giving into the temptation to, excuse the pun, fudge the numbers, disagreements will arise. And conflict is always bad for business, especially the light and sweet core business of Super Duper Land, which represents 99.99999% of our economy."

"Wait, what's the other 0.00001% then?" Inquired Ferris.

"No one really knows," answered the professor after a long pondering pause. The fox continued:

"Thus, to ensure that everything is fair and square, that geometry reference is just for you boss." Mr. Wilcox proudly paused for a moment, but his pun fell on deaf dino ears, or whatever those two small holes on the side of the Annonovosaurus' head were supposed to be. The silence obliged the fusty fox to continue with his detailed description.

"Therefore, to keep things FAIR AND SQUARE.... "Still no reaction from HRAR. "...therefore the group needs something called a central ledger. Think of it as a class attendance sheet for all the computer coins. That way when there is any funny money business, a final arbiter is there to resolve it."

"What's a arbiter? Is it like a traitorous aardvark?" asked Sherry. Ferris was sure now that she was the only other person in their party paying attention. Ryan was definitely way off in La La Land.

"Not quite your....ummm...grace. Think of an arbiter as a judge my lovely, a judge made of different rules that exist within your computer."

“But who controls the ledger? Does the group hold an election? An arm-wrestling contest? How often does the position rotate? Do two people share the responsibility? Perhaps two ledgers should be kept simultaneously, or maybe that causes more problems than it solves. Most importantly, how does the group keep whoever it chooses from asserting their own interpretation of asserting a self-proclaimed divine right of ledger-keepers and extracting rents from the proletariat?” asked Ryan to the shocking realization to Ferris that he was actually paying attention.

“That’s where the Annonovodome comes in.”

“The Annonovo what now?” asked Ferris.

“The Annonovodome is our MLAI which stands for Machine Learning and Artificial Intelligence center.”

Ferris felt the threatening pinch of looking less intelligent than his two cousins. He jumped at the opportunity to ask his own batch of smart questions.

“Interesting. I thought machine learning and artificial intelligence were one of the same?”

“Yes and no my lovely, simply put, machine learning is when we Super Duperers program our machines with sets of rules that allow them to think faster and larger than our Super Duper brains possible could. Artificial intelligence or AI is when these machines start to think for themselves by using something we like to call deep reinforcement learning.”

“Argh, I hate it when I’m forced to learn,” moaned the Major Commando.

“Yes, most Dum Dums do, but machines love learning. Especially our Annonovodome. The funny thing is, Dum Dum scientists keep on trying to preprogram these silly voices into your phones and computers. The Super Duper way is far simpler, we just modeled our AI on the brains of you Dum Dums. It turns out, you are exceptional at short term memory, probably thanks to all those selfies and tweets, but you are getting increasingly terrible at creativity and critical thinking. This is why the Annonovodome exits, it learns by feeding on the math problems you solve on a daily basis. It is the singularity of the biological Dum Dum world with the digital Super Duper world.”

“Ok, I think I am ready to sign now,” admitted Ferris. He felt utterly defeated and wanted the fast talking fox to stop blathering so that his head could stop spinning. It seemed that everyone in Annonovoburg was a fast talker.

“Excelente, just a moment, there’s the issue of the fine print, plus I need to finish the part about the distributed ledger. You see, ideally, everyone in both the Dum Dum and Super Duper world should keep their own ledger. In other words, it would be evenly distributed between everyone. But most Dum Dums simply don’t care, they want to have their cake, eat it and then post it online too. Ideally, each would have equal input and oversight when it comes to the central ledger, rather than each keeping their own. That is a daunting technical challenge for a Dum Dum citizen, but fortunately, it is one that distributed ledgers, such as our Annonovodome, has finally overcome thanks to a technology known as blockchains. Now onto the fine print…”

GROOOOOOOAN. It was a collective, single minded groan, by all three weary travelers.

“Now now Professori, you heard Sir Ferris. He is ready to sign and I’m sure he agrees to verbally waive his right to hear the fine print, which you have showed him already.” A. Rex was right, our heroes were teetering on the brink of death by boredom. Ferris was glad that the orange lizard in a top hat empathized with them. Plus, he really wanted to see this Annonovodome in person.

“Now, let me I see the form you have filled.” As the Annonovosaurus’ eyes drank up the words Ferris had scribbled neatly onto the form entitled: ‘Birthday Barter’, his greyish colored eyes widened when they came across the words: Birth Date.

“My my my,” said the pleasantly surprised orange dinosaur. “Aren’t you special?”

Chapter 18 - The Annonovodome

"Which is more fun Sir Ferris?" smirked the Annonovosaurus. "To keep a secret safe so that you and only you know the real truth, the true true story, or to share something with everyone and everything?"

"Well....if you share a secret with everyone and everything then it isn't a secret is it," replied the ever-wise knight of Bebounty.

"Excellente caliente. You are of course correct my super specimen. But I believe it is even choicer to own a secret and share it with a select few." HRAR winked playfully as he pulled open the two large pearly gates that led into the Annonovodome.

It was more super-duper than anything else in all of Super Duper Land. It was simply supercalifragilisticexpialidocious. A huge glass dome covered a wicked wonderland filled with skyrocketing roller coasters, winding water slides and arcade games galore. It was a dream come true. A promise land of perfection. The air inside smelled sweet and there were hundreds of children running around, screaming, playing and of course, eating.

"You will soon notice that the air in here has been scientifically proven to allow you to eat as much candy as you like. It was my first great invention," crowed a proud Alberti Rex. "I hope to one day own all the air in Super Duper Land."

"That's amazing exclaimed Ryan. Now not only will we never get any tummy aches ever again, we can now really eat as much as we like! Thanks Mr. Annonovo."

"No no no, thank you and thank your mother for having you on Mother's Day. As for you my dear specimen, I have something extra special for you." Ferris could feel the Annonovosaurus' claw clasp his right shoulder. It made him feel uneasy, but he was too busy taking in the sight and sounds within the Annonovodome. "If you will allow me Sir Ferris, I will place this purple pin on your lapel."

"Thank you Mr. Rex. But what does this pin do?"

"You will soon see, there," HRAR had a silly habit of sticking out his bright green tongue when trying to make use of his two scrawny hands. "Now, just say 'Hey Fafa' and let's see what happens."

Hey Fafa?" It was more of a questions, but Ferris would soon find out that it had the intended effect the Annonovosaurus was hoping for.

"Excelente callente. It's working," said A. Rex excitedly. Ferris heard a buzzing sound. He looked up and noticed a large clam shaped object hovering above them. The flying shell slowly descended and rotated slowly to face the inquisitive knight of Bebounty, right-in-between-his-four-eyes.

"Fear not Sir Ferris, this is my latest and perhaps greatest invention," assured Mr. Annonovo.

Ferris blinked cautiously at the rainbow colored mollusk. It seemed to him that the floating object was smiling back at him. The curious knight of Bebounty was just about to inch forward when a mechanical whirring sounds forced him to step back.

The clam opened, and in it, was a large shiny red spherule that Ferris soon found out fit neatly into the palm of his hand.

"Go ahead, take a bite," encouraged the orange dinosaur.

Ferris looked at the red sphere and took a big apple-sized bite. The outer shell was hard but the inside was squishy, sugary and sweet, filled with a sandy like paste that was bursting with Ferris' favorite fruity flavor - strawberry.

"Wow, that was exactly what I wanted. How on...how did it know…."

"Predictive analytics my brave knight. My latest invention actually predicts what you want before you know you want it. Isn't it genipsi!"
Mr. Annonovo had a habit of corrupting the way words were meant to be said. He pronounced the G is genius like a J. Ferris also noticed he had a nasty habit of changing the final vowel in a word to the psi sound. But these grammatical thoughts only troubled Ferris for a brief moment, he was anxious to see what the flying clam would cough up next.

"Mr. Annonovo, I have a question I've been meaning to ask you," whispered Ryan. Ferris wondered if his cousin was jealous of his new found access.

"By all means, Major Commando, go ahead,"

Are you Italian?"

"What? Oh.... because of my robe? Hea Hea Hea," laughed the Annonovosaurus loudly. His staccato laughs sounded closer to croaks. "No No, it's not the Italian flag, it's the three New Year's Eve wish colors. Unlike your world, Major Commando, Super Duper land is powered on wishes, not work. Any enterprise must have a core business, a market tested discipline that keeps the lights on. For us, that core business is wishes. We harness the energy of hope. We channel desire and aspiration. There are two types of people in this world my specimens. Those that dream and those that do. Those that lead and those that follow. There are those that tap into the darkest recesses of their mind and find the courage to persevere, then there are others that simply wish for something to happen without doing anything. Which of those two are you?"

But before either of them could answer, Mr. Annonovo Rex, the last of his kind, swung his large technicolored cape around and began walking off.

Chapter 19 - One Math Problem

Professor Wilcox promptly arrived with two crisp pieces of paper attached to large black clipboards. It was time for Ferris, Ryan and Sherry to sing for their supper (of sweets).

"Right, here is your math problem of the day, good luck. I will be back tomorrow with two more, and double the amount every day after," muttered the musty fox.

Was he really in a hurry or was he feigning being rushed?

Once again, something the fox said did not sit well with Ferris. He felt uneasy, true that was the way he had felt for most of this strange trip through Super Duper Land, but the phrase *double the amount every day after,* did not sit well with the ever attentive knight of Bebounty. Was he missing something? Professor Wilcox had stressed the same point earlier and Ferris failed to dig deeper due to the rapid and very distracting speech of the Annonovosaurus.

"Ummmm...cousin...what's six times eight again?" blurted Ryan, interrupting Ferris' trail of thought once again.

"48 doofus," it was Her Sherryness that spoke. "Don't you know your times table." She added rhetorically in between bites of a scrumptious cookie ice cream sandwich.

Ferris looked down at his own piece of paper.

9-3÷1/3+1

Please Excuse My Dear Aunt Sally.

Ferris scribbled down a nine. *That was easy* he thought. *Almost too easy.* He looked over at Sherry's page:

$$\mathbf{7 + (6 \times 5^2 + 3)}$$

Ferris noticed that Ryan was still struggling.

"Come on cousin, you got this," encouraged the astute knight of Bebounty. "Remember, PEDMAS! Start with the Parentheses:

$$\mathbf{6 \times (5 + 3) = 6 \times 8 = 48}$$

"Duh! I got that far Ferret."
"Ok chill, next you do the Exponents, then you Multiply and Divide before you Aunt Sally."

$6 \times (5 + 3) \;=\; 6 \times 8 \;=\;$ **48** Right

$6 \times (5 + 3) \;=\; 30 + 3 \;=\; 33$ (wrong)

$5 \times 2^2 \;=\; 5 \times 4 \;=\;$ **20** Right

$5 \times 2^2 = 10^2 = 100$ (wrong)

$2 + 5 \times 3 = 2 + 15 =$ **17** Right

$2 + 5 \times 3 = 7 \times 3 = 21$ (wrong)

$30 \div 5 \times 3 = 6 \times 3 =$ **18** Right

$30 \div 5 \times 3 = 30 \div 15 = 2$ (wrong)

“Thanks cuz. Wanna go ride the rollercoasters now?”

“Sure thing Ryan, let me just grab one more clam candy…”

BOOOOOOOOM!

A huge explosion erupted behind the diligently working Dum Dums. Ferris turned around and saw two scrawny children, a boy and girl, running wildly towards the gates of the Annonovodome.

“Hurry!” yelled the young boy to the girl. The little girl seemed to be limping.

Next, Ferris noticed Professor Wilcox calmly speaking into his earpiece. The horrified knight of Bebounty knew it was he who had summoned two much larger flying clams to pursue the darting duo.

"Proceed," purred the four eyed fox as the two flying clams spat out two giant pink nets that quickly brought both the little boy and little girl to the ground.

Ferris exchanged glances with Ryan. They both sprinted towards their fellow fallen Dum Dums. But before they could reach them, the little boy managed to cut himself out of the sticky net and began charging once more towards the door. It was he who was limping this time around.

While running, Ferris looked back towards Mr. Wilcox, who was calmly speaking into his wrist. He noticed one of the clams reposition itself waist high to the racing boy, it gaped open widely, and a large green lasso harpooned its way around the boy's ankles, forcing him to fall face first onto the floor, he was inches away from the entrance.

Ferris pushed on. He was far behind Ryan, who had reached the boy moments after the clam had capsized him. The out-of-breath knight of Bebounty felt his stomach starting to turn.

I thought there were no tummy aches in the Annonovodome.

Although Ryan had reached before him, Ferris sensed his legs starting to stiffen up, especially after he noticed a phalanx of Ostrich guards flank the fallen boy and his cousin.

A double encirclement strategy. Ferris felt the menace of foul play afoot. The guards dragged the boy away and shoved Ryan towards the ground. Although he couldn't make out the exact words Ryan screamed, his cousin's tone and pitch conveyed more than enough information.

"What, what happened?" asked Ferris in between breaths. He had finally caught up to the Major Commando.

"I haven't the foggiest Ferret? That poor kid just kept on repeating one thing over and over again. He looked shell shocked!"

"What?" gasped the whitewashed knight of Bebounty.

"You know, shell shocked, it's the feeling soldiers get on the battlefield, and here I thought you were the history battle buff."

"No….not that….what did he say?"

"Oh that...he just kept on repeating...Abandon All Hope....Abandon All Hope!"

Chapter 20 - Two Math Problems

"What's your earliest memory Sir Ferris?"

Ferris failed to hide his dumbstruck, deer in the headlights look. He had fallen into the Annonovosaurus' trap.

"Let you see," continued the orange dinosaur in a top hat, "had I asked this question to any normal child, they would have immediately answered their fifth, number five, birthday. It's statistically, empirically, most undoubtedly, a solid, fire born, fact," he chuckled while fanning out five of the six fingers that erupted out of claws.

Ferris could not really recollect. He was too busy focusing on his hosts yellow stained teeth. His eyes crawled all over the Annonovosaurus' scaly skin like an ant at a picnic. Ferris paused at the three golden dots underneath the reptiles left eye, they reminded him of the three stars he usually saw outside his bedroom during moonless night over Kay City.

"Enough with the riddles A. Rex. We demand answers!" shouted Ryan.

"Precisely my dear Major Commando. An analogy is the best kind of answer. That poor unfortunate soul you just witnessed had an issue with his memory. That's all you see. Nothing more to it."

"Where did he come from?" asked Sherry.

“Come from….errr…” It was obviously to Ferris that Mr. Annonovo was stalling. Something again did not sit right with the righteous knight of Bebounty.

“He seemed to be stuck in the Annonovodome’s underground cooling system,” chimed Mr. Wilcox. “The Annonovodome uses an ancient cooling method called a Qanat. Gills covering the glass dome above catch cool air which is sucked down through a series of vertical access shafts by a stream water that is gently sloping underground. This is the water we use to make the delicious candy you so crave. It’s all organic and natural I assure thee.”

“But what about the explosion?” Ferris finally spoke.

“Substitutiary locomotion. Mystic power that's far beyond the wildest notion. It's a weird so feared, yet wonderful to see.”

What on earth is this cloak covered fool blathering on about.

“Now now my specimens….” continued the Annonovosaurs. “You mustn't concern yourselves with these trivial matters. Have you tried out our latest AR/VR stations? They won’t be released in Japan for another three years. I call them Neural Nets.” Mr. Rex quickly fished out two hat-like pieces of white cloth from the inner pockets of his long coat. He was wearing a black, velvety, robe today. Ferris noted that black was indeed the absence of color.

Ryan reached out. He grabbed the shriveled up white netty cloth and slowly covered his head. His hair was ensnared and the white rim of the Neural Net made his forehead look twice as large.

"Don't you dare laugh Ferret," he threatened defensively. "Come on then, let's give it a go."

Ryan knew how to push Ferris over the limit. He had done so countless times before. He was an expert at navigating the avolitious knights of Bebounty's razor's edge of timidity. It was blowing giant bubbles at the beach house all over again.

Come to think of it, Ferris did feel like a modern day Alice, trapped in a twisted wonderland. *So did that make Ryan the white rabbit?*

"Today, Sir Ferris, today," egged on the Major Commando. "Or are you too clucking scared to try?" The final push had been administered, masterfully.

"Give me that," grumbled the goaded knight of Bebounty. The Neural Net seemed harmless enough. It was stretchy and the fabric felt well knit. *Like a pair of underwear for the head. Why do they call it a pair of underwear?*

Ferris carefully covered his head. He imagined he looked as silly as his cousin did.

"Excellente caliente," growled the Annonovosaurus. "Hold onto your bottompsi."

It was instant. Ferris and Ryan were no longer in the Annonovodome. They were somewhere else entirely.

Ferris' gaze was immediately transfixed on a large layered structure in the distance. It was firetruck red and crowned by a large spire pointing perilously towards a grey cloud covered sky. The roof looked like a picnic blanket being laid down in slow motion, except that there was some anti-gravitational force preventing it from lying flat. In fact, there were about seven different picnic blankets stacked up one after the other. Ferris felt a sudden craving for red-velvet pancakes.

"Woaaaaah. Where on earth are we?" gasped Ryan.

Earth?

"Were in some computer generated dream world cousin."

"Wow, it's so.... mystic."

Any sufficiently advanced technology is indistinguishable from magic.

"*Teishi shimasu!*"

Ferris whirled backwards and immediately noticed two giant golden antlers rising from the six concentric copper circles forming the center of a large reddish-gold helmet. Both the helmet and the roof of the Shinto shrine seemed to share a certain design quality. They both appeared to be fluid even though they were probably both made from sturdy stuff. But then again, was any of this truly real?

"*Shikibetsu!*"

The fear Ferris felt was real enough.

"Cool, we must be in Japan. Ancient Japan by the looks of it. A. Rex did mention that this thing was being built for the Japanese market."

Ferris barely heard anything Ryan said. His eyes had made their way past the Samurai's helmet and were now drawn towards the hips of the armored soldier. Ferris was alarmed by how large the Samurai's hands were, his senses were heightened, by witnessing the warrior slowly unsheathing his sword.

"Um Ryan, I don't think we're supposed to be here. I think..."

"Ōheina buta!"

The sequence of events that followed were so fast that Ferris felt a lag between what his eyes were perceiving in front of him and the sound that came a few seconds later. Was it a lag in the Neural Net software or were the Samurai's movements so rapid that they overcame the speed of sound? It was probably a mixture of both, but the temporized knight of Bebounty was thankful that the Major Commando Mega Jumbo had his axe at the ready.

Ryan tarried the katana's swing with the belly of his axe and charged his shoulder into the samurai's breastplate. Steel sang on steel as the two battled furiously for what seemed like an eternity. Ferris noticed that his cousin was dressed in an all-black jumpsuit. The Major Commando had become a nefarious ninja and was briskly closing in on the giant samurai like a long night. Ryan had kicked and shoved the warrior into a corner before easily knocking him and his katana down to the ground. Ferris noticed that the ground was white, covered in, thousands of white flowers.

Cherry blossoms.

“Finish him!” Ferris found himself yelling in exhilaration.

“Ahhhhhhhh!” Ryan joined in on the screaming, raising his axe high above his head as he jumped ten feet into the air. Ferris noticed that his cousin was suspended in mid motion for what felt like forever before he came crashing back down, with the toe of his axe leading the way.

Ferris felt the large helmet come crashing down as well. The cherry blossoms beneath it slowly turned from white to red.

****

“That was awesome!” piqued Ryan.

“Well done Major Commando. I hope Lord General Honda Tadakatsu wasn’t too much of a handful?” asked Mr. Annonovo.

“Not at all Mr. Rex! I got him good didn’t I?”

“You’re a regular Jack Merridew my specimen. Sir Ferris, why did you not engage in battle?”

Ferris was still titillating from the trip through the Neural Net. “I, I think I’ve had enough battles for a lifetime. In fact,

I think I've had enough of this whole place. Ryan, I think it's time to go home."

"Home? But why? We only just got here yesterday!" belched Ryan.

"The Major Commando is correct my dear knight of Bebounty. Plus, we have a contract. Professori Wilcox, would you be so kind so as to remind these two gentlemen of their accord and furnish them with their problem sets of the day."

"Roger wilco Mr. Rex. Two problems coming right up!"

Chapter 21 - Compounding Interests

Ferris could feel a sharp pain streaking across the palm of his hand. The pain was much more than the pain he felt writing one of his many had written apology letters to his mum back in Kay City. Ferris was famous for sliding these letters under the door of the living room. He found the soft power of a written apology worked wonders on adults. He wondered, if his official letter of complaint to the Annonovosaurus would have the same effect.

It was day five or six of their time in the Annonovodome. The days all seemed to jumble up together and both of his cousins had grown weary. You see, on the third day (the first day after the explosion) the sly Professor Wilcox had brought each of the three travelers a set of four math problems each. Ferris made easy work of that, although he did also have to help out both Ryan and Sherry with their trigonometry. On Day Four, Ferris was alarmed to see that the pesky lab coat clad fox had brought a problem set with a total of eight math questions.

"What in tarnation is going on here. Now just a minute," Ryan had started. But Mr. Wilcox casually pointed to the fine print, which plainly explained that:

'Signatories of the Birthday Barter Charter in exchange for products and services rendered must perform to their best ability a previously agreed upon number of mathematical problems per day starting with one problem on the first number day, followed a doubling of the number of problems each day after ad infinitum.'

Ferris found out that *ad infinitum* was just fancy way of saying forever and double forever was certainly a long time. He had also found out that the Annonovodome was actually more like an iceberg than a dome in that the vast majority of the birthday bartering children from the Dum Dum world were actually housed, or better yet, trapped underground across nine different levels. Each level was filled with hundreds if not thousands of children who had made the treacherous journey across Super Duper Land in hopes of a better life by trading their birthday away. The first subterranean level consisted of boys and girls who were considered good kids. They simply believed they were misunderstood. They did all their homework and problem sets on time and rarely complained. They may have forgotten to raise their hand in class before asking a question or may have stood for too long in front of the TV while their parents were watching a movie. The second level, was full of children who craved the toys and candy of others. They were blown about in a violent storm and some were even forced to do their math problems hanging upside down. The third level was reserved for those kids that ate too much. Despite the fact that the settlers of the Annonovodome never got a tummy ache, there was a clause within the contract that prevented them from overeating. These gluttons were buried neck up in a cold slush like liquid. The fourth level, Ferris soon found out, was reserved for two constantly warring groups of children. The children who preferred to hoard their candy and the children that constantly grabbed as many candies as they could off the shelf of super markets. Ferris heard that they were constantly jousting and warring with one another, pushing giant gumballs back and forth. These giant gumballs would stick to whatever candy was left lying around from the hoarders or the shelvers, allowing each gumball to then snowball into epic proportions. The fifth underground level was the level at which the cool liquid that made up the Qanat system of the Annonovodome ran its course. This level was reserved for bad tempered children that readily threw tantrums. As their punishment, they would have to do math problems while drifting in a boat with hole in it. Some would be busy scribbling while others would be busy trying to plug up the holes or toss out buckets full of water. The sixth sub terrestrial level was reserved for naughty children who too easy fibbed their way out of sticky situations. This level worried Ferris the most as his mum frequently reminded him that a lie of omission, meaning lying by not denying something that someone attributes to you, is just as terrible as an actual blatant lie.

"Arrrrrrrggggghhhhhh!"

A large moan echoed up the air around the deep thinking knight of Bebounty, breaking his trail of thought. It was a Mega Jumbo groan. Ferris glanced over and noticed Professor Wilcox handing over a thick problem set to his cousin Ryan. The putrid fox then casually skipped over towards the cross legged knight of Bebounty.

"Here you go Sir Ferris. Your problem set for the day."

Ferris quickly counted the number of questions. Sixteen! That must mean that it was still only day five of their escapade and that tomorrow would be the start of an exponential nightmare.

"Thank you Mr. Wilcox. Please note that I am hereby officially submitting a Letter of Grievance for violations of the terms set forth within our contract."

"What?" gasped the greasy fox. "What violations?"

Ferris imagined the sounds of a violin playing as he chose his next words wisely.

“The violations are all clearly stated in my letter. I suggest you share it immediately with your employer so that we may pursue the next necessary course of action.”

“Very well, now here…” yelled the fox as he shoved the clipboard into Ferris’ face. “Do your work.”

Ferris calmly placed the stack of sheets on the floor next to him. He then decided to pen a quick letter to an old fiery friend. This letter he would deliver by pigeon post, the only permissible method of contact between the outside world and the Annonovodome. It wasn’t the fastest way to get a message out of Annonovoburg, but Ferris hoped that it would reach his fellow knight in time.

****

“How dare you accuse me of foul play, you…you puny specimen. I’ll have you know that my reputation precedes me. All the birds and the bees of Super Duper Land and all its citizens praise my goodly nature. I am an inventor. I am an entrepreneur. I am a statesman. A captain of both industry and sky. I am the most learned.”

It was obvious to Ferris that his letter had triggered some deep insecurity buried within one Alberti R. Annonovo.

“Mr. Rex. The aim of my letter was not meant to offend. It was simply a phenomenological statement of facts. If you wish for us to deliberate the contents further, then may I suggest a more proper venue?” Well said by the calm, well-spoken, knight of Bebounty.

“My my, poor be the pupil who does not surpass his master. It is you who will be giving the orders now I see?”

BANG! The Annonovosaurus jumped on his coco blanco desk and let out a huge roar.

ROOOOOOOAAAARRRRRR!

Trying his best to control his irascibility and compose himself, Mr. Rex continued:

“Fine, state the name of the place you wish for us to arbitrate the matter further.”

“The High Court of Lollipolis.”

“Too far, choose again.”

“Then I choose the Supreme Court of Super Duper Land.”

“That’s even further, and any grievances must be first cleared up by a local county court, therefore, I say we set the trial for our own very County Court of Annonovoburg,” smirked the orange dinosaur as he stepped down off of his desk. “If needs be, you could then easily follow the due process and appeal in either of the two aforementioned courts. Do we have an accord?”

Ferris felt that he had no choice but to try his chances at the county court. He shook the Annonovosaurus’ scrawny claw vigorously as he silently wished he was back at the beach house or overlooking the bay by Kay City, counting boats.

Chapter 22 - Makoto

The county court of Annonovoburg was a small decrepit building. Its design was a stark contrast to the ultramodern Annonovodome and the rustic yet breathtaking Castle De Annonovo. It was sand colored, with the paint slowly chipping away at the edges of the walls and the roof. A single floored building, the edifice housed three separate courtrooms, two small and one larger than the two small ones combined. The small court room on the right of the building had a sign labeled: 'Civil Court' while the opposite (mirror image) room had a sign labeled: 'Claims Court.' Ferris and his two cousins were ushered into the central room which had a sign that read: 'Court of Appeals'.

Finally, Ferris thought. He felt at ease that they were heading to the right place to plead their case.

Professor Wilcox led the procession of Ostrich guards surrounding the three travelers from the Dum Dum world into the main courtroom. He drew them down the middle and stopped at the end by facing a large wooden bench.

"That's where the judge sits," whispered Ryan.

"Shhhhh," countered Sherry. "Don't you know that you have to be quiet in a courtroom doofus!"

The laconic knight of Bebounty did not partake in his cousins' frivolous banter. He considered it jejune and was too focused on the opening statement he had just finished writing that very morning. Ferris did however notice, that the benches behind them were filled with the various birds, bees and blue pigs that they had encountered throughout their journey from Bubblegum City to Annonovoburg. He also noticed, that the treacherous Annonovosaurus was sitting on the bench across from the central aisle, sitting with his two large legs crossed and filing his long black claws. Mr. Rex had opted to wear a long white fur coat this afternoon, complete with a tall white furry top hat.

"All rise, the honorable Judge Jack K. Hopper presiding."

Ferris could not believe his eyes. Judge Hopper was nothing more than a tall, broad shouldered, grey kangaroo draped in a black robe.

A Kangaroo Court!

The restrained knight of Bebounty could feel his blood boil. Ferris decided to take a deep breath to try and compose himself. After all, the knight's code of Rei or Respect was all about not jumping, or in this case, hopping, into conclusions. Besides, Judge Hopper seamed seasoned enough, especially since his silver spectacles hanged half way between his snout edge and his eye line.

"Please be seated," coughed the elderly kangaroo. "Bailiff, has the defense been provided proper counsel in lieu of the proceedings and where is the prosecution?"

Ferris managed a smile as he noticed that the bailiff was a neatly dressed brown bear. The eagle-eyed knight of Bebounty noticed that the bailiff's badge clearly represented the virtue of Gi or Integrity. That revelation managed to calm Ferris down even further.

"Yes your honor," answered the bearish bailiff. "The prosecution should be arriving any moment."

Prosecution? But what about my opening statement?

Just as Ferris was getting ready to object, the two large wooden doors of the Annonovoburg Court of Appeals swung open.

"Apologies, apologies your honor. We were in the wrong courtroom. I don't think we have had an appeals case ever since this building was first built by Henry the VIII, or was it the Henry the VI of House Annonovo? My memory isn't what it used to be. I see that the defendant is here. Hello Baron Alberti, so great to see you again my lord."

Ferris turned around. Once again, Super Duper land was full of surprises.

"Ummmm....hell no!" shouted Sherry. His cousin had taken the words right out of the muted knight of Bebounty's mouth. "And why is he the defendant, we're the victims here!"

"Ya, no way we are letting a bunch of puppets do the talking for us," added Ryan.

Ferris glanced over at the Annonovosaurus who was trying his best to suppress a satisfying chuckle while pretending to continue to examine his claws.

"Order, order...*cough cough!*" gasped the honorable Judge Jack K. Hopper as he struck a large wooden gavel on his desk.

“Your honor, if I may approach the bench,” asked Ferris politely.

“Permission, *cough!*, granted Sir Ferris.”

“Thank you your honor.” Ferris knew that he had to stay calm, composed and most importantly, confident. He was proud that he carried himself well towards the judge’s towering bench, he even slyly nudged aside the two prosecution puppets who were no doubt arranged by the Annonovosaurus.
“Your honor, might you permit me to represent myself and my fellow Dum Dum world visitors. I believe this is custom with the laws of Super Duper Land which provide us immigrant visitors full rights of enfranchisement. I can see that the defendant, Mr. Alberti R. Annonovo Rex is due to represent his own interests in person. Therefore, by Newton’s Third Law which clearly states that ‘for every action, there is an equal and opposite reaction,’ we, your honor, must reserve the right to self-representation.”

“Eloquently put Sir Ferris. However, I strongly suggest you retain your counsel, if only to consult with them on the intricacies of our by-laws and executive orders.”

“Of course.”

“Then this court recognizes the preference of the plaintiff to represent the interests of himself, Major Commando Mega Jumbo and Princess Her Sherryness in the case of Sir Ferris Bebounty of Kay City vs. Baron Alberti R. Annonovo Rex of Annonovoburg. Sir Ferris, please state your case, clearly, before the court.” The judge then cleared his own throat in the most awkward of ways.

Surprisingly, Ferris did not feel at all nervous. He was prepared and ready to parrot away the opening statement he had prepared.

"Your honor, ladies and gentlemen of the jury, people of majestic Annonovoburg and citizens of Super Duper Land. Peace be upon you all. As a visitor in this wonderful land I have been constantly tossed between bouts of exhilaration and extreme fear. I recognize your calling to greatness and I have been inspired by the spurring metropoli you have built and the meiyo by which you pursue even the seemingly most menial of tasks. You are truly super-duper in every letter of the phrase."

Ferris decided to pause for effect. He quickly scanned the jury and noticed that it was too filled with puppets and piglets of various sizes and colors. He carried on nevertheless with his speech.

"Letters. Our case today is contingent on our understanding of letters. Letters and numbers both the single and the several that make up a standard birthday barter contract which has been used countless times before by that dastardly dino defendant. My task today is simple, it is to prove to you, beyond the shadow of a single or several doubt, that we three Dum Dum citizens have been swindled, hoodwinked and bamboozled by Baron De Annonovo, his crew and his caboodle. Justice, ladies and gentlemen, will today flow like the stream beneath the Annonovodome and set free the very fiber of freedom - the truth."

Chirp. Chirp. Chirp.

Ferris was flabbergasted. He at least expected a few gratifying claps here and there, but all he could hear were the deafening chirps of crickets. He knew that this was but the first round of deliberation and decided to cut himself some slack. He knew it was important to save both his energy and his composure for the next bout.

"Thank you Sir Ferris, the court recognizes the defendant, Baron Alberti R. Annonovo Rex, do you wish to make an opening statement Mr. Rex."

The last Annonovosaurus had by then adjusted himself and was now sitting erect in his seat. His trusted, diamond encrusted, cane twirling casually by his side.

"Not at this time your honor."

HRAR's casual disposition caused great alarm to the calculating knight of Bebounty. *No opening statement. Perhaps my move to represent myself was too masterful for that dummersaurus. Advantage Ferris!*

"Very well, Sir Ferris, your first witness."

"Actually your honor, I call no witnesses…"

There was a large unexpected gasp in the courtroom which startled Sir Ferris into stopping his speech.

"Order, order!" assured the judge. "Sir Ferris, please continue."

“Thank you your honor. As I was saying, I call no witnesses today, for my only witness is justice herself.”

Chirp. Chirp. Chirp.

Ferris could not help but feel frustration brewing. Of all the times he had replayed that particular phrase in his mind, he always imagined either a large gasp, similar to the one that just interrupted him, or rambunctious cheers to follow.

“Your honor, we the people would like to enter Exhibit A into evidence.” Ferris nodded to Ryan, who immediately unfolded a large sheet of paper which he carefully stuck onto a easel slanted nonchalantly in between the judges desk and the jury.

“The jury will recognize Exhibit A brought forth by the plaintiff. Please proceed Sir Ferris and mind you, with haste.”

“Of course your honor. Ladies and gentle-stooges of the jury. Exhibit A is the only piece of proof that I need to state my case. It is the ultimate clause in our contract with Mr. Annonovo Rex. This clause clearly states that:

‘Signatories of the Birthday Barter Charter in exchange for products and services rendered must perform to their best ability a previously agreed upon number of mathematical problems per day starting with one problem on the ***<u>first number day</u>****, followed a doubling of the number of problems each day after ad infinitum.’*

Notice, that I have underlined and bolded the phrase ‘first number day’ as this is our main point of contention.”

"Sir Ferris, I better see where this is going soon," warned the judge curtly.

"Most certainly your honor. The defendant assumes that the phrase first number actually refers to the number 1 and therefore a doubling of the number 1 is 2 and a doubling of 2 is 4 and so on and so forth."

"We are all aware of basic mathematics Sir Ferris. Please state your point clearly," pleaded the grey kangaroo.

"Well, this is where the defendant is wrong your honor. Wrong I say. Wrong since the first contract signed. The first number, as anybody can attest, is the number 0...not the number 1."

Chirp. Chirp. Chirp.

Ferris carried on. "Thenceforth, double of 0 is 0 and double of 0 is 0 again, each day after ad infinitum!"

"Objection your honor," screamed the no longer quiet Baron of Annonovoburg.

"Overruled. Mr. Annonovo, I am as shocked at this revelation as you are, but the letters, as Sir Ferris so eloquently put it, are staring us back loud and clear. I have no option but to overrule your objection. You may state your case during the closing argument of course. Sir Ferris, do you have any further evidence to add or does the prosecution rest its case?"

"Yes your honor. But before the prosecution rests, I have one more claim to make."

"Proceed."

"Your honor, in my opening statement, I mentioned that throughout this trip, I felt constantly tossed between bouts of exhilaration and extreme fear. Well, in addition, I have been constantly teetering on the edge of truth and dishonestly. Alas, today and before all who are here and before one special friend who isn't, I would like to openly claim in this court, that I am no knight."

This time there was a huge gasp. Ferris felt somewhat satisfied but mostly wanted to yell out:
Oh that gets the big reaction! But he didn't speak his mind. Instead, he continued to speak from his heart.

"I have learned a great deal about the virtues of knighthood throughout our journey across this Super Duper Land. I learned about the importance of Chu or loyalty to my fellow travelers. I discovered that Meiyo or honor means more off the battlefield than on it. I falsely exhibited six of the seven virtues of knighthood and today, I would like to exhibit the seventh and my first true virtue. Makoto. For one cannot truly belong to the brotherhood of knighthood if he is not at first honest with himself as well as with others. From now on, may the hallowed Owl be my sigil as it should be the symbol of this trial. There you have it. I revoke my title of Sir and remain forever yours, Ferris the Furious, aspiring knight of Bebounty. Thank you your honor, ladies and gentlemen of the jury. The prosecution rests its case."

Speaking of numbers, Ferris was on cloud nine. He glided back to sit squarely in between his two cousins. Ryan extended his fist and Ferris felt immense joy as he bumped the corner of the Major Commando's fist with his. *Well done* mouthed Sherry. The virtuous (one out of seven is a start at least) knight of Bebounty finally felt at ease.

Chapter 23 - Promethean Fire

"Mr. Annonovo, your closing statement if you please?" invited Judge Hopper.

Unfrazzled, Baron Alberti R. Annonovo Rex, stood up and began his soliloquy.

"Thousands of years ago, the first Annonovosaurs, Prometheus Prime Rex, discovered how to make fire. He was probably burned at the stake he had taught his brothers to light. He was considered an evildoer who had dealt with a demon dinokind dreaded. But thereafter all of Super Duper Land had fire to keep them warm, to make their famous candy, to light their caves. He had left them a gift they had not conceived and he had lifted the darkness off of our world. Centuries later, another Annonovosaurus invented the wheel. He was probably torn on the rack he had taught his brothers to build. He was considered a transgressor who ventured into forbidden territory. But thereafter, citizens of this great land could travel past any horizon. He had left them a gift they had not conceived and he had opened the roads of the world."

"Throughout the centuries there were countless other Annononovosauri who took first steps down new roads armed with nothing but their own vision. Their goals differed, but they all had this in common: that the step was first, the road new, the vision unborrowed, and the response they received—hatred. The great creators—the thinkers, the artists, the scientists, the inventors—stood alone against the Dum Dums of their time. Every great new thought was opposed. Every great new invention was denounced. The first motor was considered foolish. The teleporter was considered impossible. The Annonovodome was considered vicious. But the men of unborrowed vision went ahead. They fought, they suffered and they paid. But they won."

"No creator was prompted by a desire to serve the Dum Dum world, for the Dum Dum world rejects the gifts offered and that gift destroyed the slothful routine of their lives. His truth was his only motive. His own truth, and his own work to achieve it in his own way. A symphony, a book, an engine, a philosophy, an airplane or a building—that was his goal and his life. Not those who heard, read, operated, believed, flew or inhabited the thing he had created. The creation, not its users. The creation, not the benefits others derived from it. The creation which gave form to his truth. He held his truth above all things and against all."

"His vision, his strength, his courage came from his own spirit. Creators are not selfless. It is the whole secret of their power—that it was self-sufficient, self-motivated, self-generated. A first cause, a fount of energy, a life force, a prime mover. The creator served nothing and no one. He lives for himself. And only by living for himself was he able to achieve the things which are the glory of Super Duper Land. Such is the nature of achievement."

"My act of loyalty is to every creator who ever lived and was made to suffer by the force responsible, to every tortured hour of loneliness, denial, frustration, abuse he was made to spend—and to the battles he won. To every creator whose name is known—and to every creator who lived, struggled and perished unrecognized before he could achieve. To every creator who was destroyed in body or in spirit."

"I am no chrysostom charlatan. I am an Annonovosaurus who does not exist for others."

There were no sounds of crickets when Baron Alberti R. Annonovo Rex, the last of his kind, came to the end of his closing statement. The courtroom was filled by loud and hectic cheers that almost blew the rickety roof off. The applause were deafening and Ferris was left spellbound.

"Order in the court...order!" yelled Judge Hopper. "Does the defense rest its case?"

HRAR answered with his signature smile. "Yes your honor, nothing further."

"Ladies and gentlemen of the jury. You have heard both sides of the case. Have you come to a verdict?"

A short blue pig lady stood up. She was wearing a red polka dot hood. "We have your honor; we the people find the Baron Alberti R. Annonovo Rex...NOT GUILTY.

Ferris felt the world around him grow dark and silent. Everything was moving in slow motion. He noticed his cousin Ryan banging his fists on the desk, screaming the same soundless scream he usually screams underwater. He saw his other cousin, Sherry, bury her head into her folded arms, her hands, clutching Hungry Bunny tightly. The shell-shocked knight of Bebounty turned to see the Annonovosaurus smiling widely and repetitively petting his left palm with his right claw. Ferris closed his eyes, his bubble of troubles was too big to blow away. He knew his only option was to burst his inner rage wide open.

ROOOOOOOOOOOOOOOAR!

Ferris was as shocked as the rest of the courtroom. He never knew that he could roar so loudly.

ROOOOOOOOOOOOOOOAR! *There it was again*, but this time, Ferris' lips did not even move. The baffled knight of Bebounty turned around. It was a sight for sore eyes.

"Blaze! You're back."

ROOOOOOOOOOOOOOAR!

"That I am my fellow knight. I got your letter. Seems that I have arrived just in the nick of..."

"Seize them!" yelled the Annonovosaurus. "They have a contract to honor!"

"Over my dead body" assured Sir Blaze as he jumped across the aisle and planted himself in between the two desks that separated Ferris, Ryan and Sherry from the HRAR and his Ostrich guards. You see, chocodragons were much larger than either ostriches or Annonovosauruses, so there was no doubt that Mr. Alberti R. Annonovo Rex would need to take a few steps back.

The dragonknight continued. "This Kangaroo Court has come to its natural conclusion. Everyone move along now. The Dum Dums will be coming with me. I hereby declare this court in contempt of itself."

"What! How dare you insult the very foundation of rule, the essence of all our laws in Super Duper Land" grumbled Mr. Rex. "I see that you dragons are all the same, you only understand brute force. Thankfully, as an entrepreneur extraordinaire, I am always one to prepare. Professori Wilcox! Summon in my mercenary Griffin guard!"

That certainly piqued the interest of Sir Blaze.

"Isn't that your mortal enemy?" asked Ryan "Shall we assume our battle positions?"

"No Major Commando, this is a battle I must face alone. You and Sherry go open the gates of the Annonovodome and set your fellow citizens free. It's time to cut the temperature."

Judge Jack Hopper had been observing the events in front of him unfold, quietly, from the safety of his elevated desk. *I'm getting too old for this*, he thought, as he gently polished his spectacle using his gown. His ears however, were erect with alert as he heard something stomping its way towards the back of his desk. Judge Hopper knew he had to find that youthful strength to jump up over his desk and hop down the aisle, far away from the madness that was surely about to ensure.

"See you blokes later," chimed Judge Hopper as he found himself planted in between Sir Blaze and Mr. Rex. "Alberti, it's been a pleasure serving in your court, but I believe it's time that I retired. Toodles!"

The Annonovosaurus was too busy staring down Sir Blaze to even acknowledge one word of what Judge Hopper said before he hopped his way out of the courtroom.

"Prepare to die clumsy dragon." threatened HRAR.

Sir Blaze was prepared with the best response. "Never wish for death, nor fear his might!"

BOOOOOOOOOOOOOOOOOOOM!

"Well, well, well. If It isn't Sir Poof the Fireless Dragon," taunted the griffin as he dusted bits and pieces of the courtroom wall and judges desk off of his wings and shoulders. Ferris noticed that the griffin has a similarly sharp beak like the Rukh did. He also noticed how the rest of his body was a much larger version of the lioness and that his wings were scaly the same way the Twydra's body was. This uber menace was basically a compilation of all the nasty monsters they had previously faced.

Just the simple sight of the griffin made Blaze's blood boil. "Hello Garry, it's been a while," began the dragonknight. "You are not getting under my skin this time. This time. I have my friend Ferris to thank. For he has reminded me of the virtues of Rei and Makoto. I have finally admitted to myself that I have a hot head and that I have trouble respecting my enemies, no matter how pathetic they are. Therefore, in the name of Rei I salute thee."

The griffin watched in disbelief as Sir Blaze furnished him with the salute of Super Duper Land. Mr. Annonovo Rex was also shocked at the sight. He had never seen such a demonstration of respect for one's foe.

"Enough with the pleasantries you two." howled Alberti R. Annonovo Rex. "Destroy him!"

Chapter 24 - Finding the Fire Within

Gary the Griffin was no slouch. He had come prepared and was wielding his favorite weapon - a flail. A flail was a spiky ball attached to a wooden rod. It is also commonly known as a mace-and-chain. The gargantuan griffin also carried a large round shield emblazoned with a black shadow of his likeness (a side profile) on a purple field. Gary's head was covered in a blue horned helmet with two large coils covering either side of the helmet and ending in two large parallel points.

Sir Blaze was too armed and ready, with a trusted large broad axe and brown shield. The two giants squared off, watching each other's every step, taunting each other with every movement, their weapons banging across their shields.

It was Gary who made the first move. The griffin rotated his flail loudly above his head before crashing it down on Sir Blazes shield, which splintered wood everywhere as the spikes scrapped across. Both Messers Rex and Wilcox cheered in delight as the griffin then charged the dragonknight using the edge of his purple shield which was met with the cheek of Sir Blaze's axe. Steel sang on steel as Sir Blaze crashed the blade of his axe into the griffin's helmet.

"Is that all you got?" heckled Garry. "Felt a bit of a tickle."

Blaze planted his feet squarely before charging.

"Arrrrrrrgh!"

The griffin was ready for the wyverian onslaught. He had crouched down on all fours and had spread his wings widely in order to meet the great force of Sir Blaze's collision Grabbing the dragon by the waist side, Garry started to flap his wings maniacally, lifting both bodies high into the air and through the roof of the courthouse. Debris rained down everywhere as Ferris, Mr. Rex and Mr. Wilcox arched their heads upwards, shielding their eyes as best they could whilst trying to get a glimpse of the warring beasts.

THUDDDDDD!

Ferris was alarmed to see that the griffin had gotten the upper hand by ploughing his knee deep into the breastplate of the fallen dragonknight. Blaze was clearly out of breath and was struggling to set himself free from under the griffin's dastardly grasp.

"Finish him!" yelled the ever impatient Annonovosaurus Rex.

Ferris noticed the griffin menacingly rotating his flail once more. The electrified knight of Bebounty was thrown into a deeper pit of dismay when he realized that the griffin had somehow unmasked his fellow knight. Sir Blaze's head was now clearly exposed and made an easy target for the spiky ball at the end of the griffin's chain.

"NOOOOOOOOO!"

It was pure instinct. Ferris had found the Yu and the Meiyo to grab Sir Blaze's shield and propel his body in between the dragon's face and the falling mace. The full weight of the flail fell squarely on the shielded knight of Bebounty casting him clear across the courtroom.

“Sir Ferrisssssss,” screamed the dragonknight as a great flame erupted from his nostrils, blinding the griffin and forcing the colossal half-eagle half lion monstrosity off of him.

“Ferris,” yelled Ryan and Sherry almost in unison. The pair had returned with a rafter of other children from the Dum Dum world. The Major Commando was itching to get into battle but was dissuaded by Sir Blaze holding out the palm of his hand as he carefully shuffled his way towards the fallen knight of Bebounty.

There he was, Ferris was laying spread eagle on the courtroom floor. So frail, so fragile, so lifeless. Sir Blaze saw nothing but red.

“Gaaaarry!” screamed the dragonknight. It was a scream that shook every onlooker to their very core. The griffin was still blinded by the fire booger blast. He was now about to get roasted.

Sir Blaze fixed his gaze towards the discombobulated griffin and coldly stated: “May my flame purify your lost soul!”

Alberti R. Annonovo Rex had never seen a mightier display in all his life. Wave upon wave of molten combustion covered the griffin from helmet to toe, igniting all his feather at once in a twisting firestorm of immense pain. The shrills and shrieks made by the burning beast were deafening as the griffin somehow found a way to get airborne before crashing down in the distance a few farsangs away from the courthouse. Mr. Annonovo Rex knew he had been defeated and that it was time to slowly remove himself from the situation. It was now or never as the chocodragon seemed to be preoccupied with his fallen comrade, who was also joined by his two cousins and a few dozen birthday barterers.

“Willllllllcox!” The sniveling professor had already beaten him to it. HRAR quietly swore that the treacherous fox would soon pay for his insolence, but presently, Baron Alberti R. Annonovo Rex, the last of his kind, was only concerned with leaving this whole mess behind.

Chapter 25 - Return to Kay City

Ferris slowly recovered to find an all too familiar sight in front of him. There was his best friend Ryan, Major Commando Mega Jumbo, his other cousin, Princess Her Sherryness and his idol and savior, Sir Blaze Barras-Hargan, staring back down at him.

"Good show old sport! You had me worried there for a second," whispered Sir Blaze endearingly.

"Now that's what I call Yu!" added the Major Commando.

"My hero," cheered the Princess Her Sherryness.

"Come on guys, it was all pure feeling. I don't actually remember doing anything."

"Enough with the Makoto Sir Ferris. You have earned your knighthood today. On this same glorious day as I have earned my stripes back. See?" The dragonknight proudly pointed at the three red and yellow striped adorning his broad brown shoulders.

"Well done Sir Blaze," commended Ferris. "And I am no knight. I lied to you this entire trip."

"Aye, you may have omitted the truth as you said in this here court, but you found the courage to be honest with yourself in the end. A knight's journey of virtue is not about how you start, but where you finish. Therefore, it is my pleasure to knight thee Sir Ferris Bebounty, Knight of Dragonhood."

"Dragonhood?" inquired the ever earful and perhaps slightly jealous Major Commando.

"Aye Dragonhood, that's where all dragonknights are from."

"Oh, so he is a dragonknight now, is he?" asked Her Sherryness

"Yes your grace. One of the finest I have ever seen."

Ferris sensed tension arising. He knew it was his duty to make sure that calmer heads prevailed, especially since he really had no fight left in him after those epic battles.

"Sir Blaze, are there any trophies you could perhaps bestow on my dear cousin, Major Commando Mega Jumbo? I would not be here without him you know?"

"Why of course," replied the chocodragon. "Ummmm.... how about this Golden Spear of Destiny?" mumbled Sir Blaze as he picked up one of the two spires that formerly crowned the helmet of the fallen griffin.

"Oh wow" exclaimed the theatrical knight of Bebounty. "The Spear of Destiny you say?"

"You Dum Dums think I don't know what you're doing? I'm not a child..." Ryan's face looked super serious for a moment..." but, I'll take it. For I am Major Commando Mega Jumbo of House Razzmatazz and Keeper of the Spear of Destiny. Now what about all the other formerly trapped children at the Annonovodome?"

“Freedom is the greatest gift of all.” Ferris knew Sir Blaze was right. It did feel good to finally be free.

“Hoorah,” led Sir Blaze in cheer. Three cheers for the three weary travelers. “Hip hip…”

All the Dum Dums replied in unison. “Hooray”

“Hip hip…”

“...Hooray”

“Hip hip…”

“...Hooray!”

“Marshmellous, now, who wants a lift back to Bubblegum City?” concluded the dragonknight.

****

Back at the beach house in Kay City. All was calm, all was quiet. Ferris, Ryan and Sherry had tumbled out of the TV and into the living room. All the adults were strangely still asleep.

“Wow, feels great to be back! Doesn’t it cousin?” exclaimed Ryan.

“It sure does Major Commando. Sherry, are you ok?”

“Yes I am Sir Ferris, and Hungry Bunny is in one piece as well.”

“Terrific, do you think we could stop with the Super Duper names already? It feels kinda silly now that we are back at Kay by the Bay.”

“What’s the matter dragonknight, too much fun in the Super Duper sun?” teased Ryan.

“More than enough for a lifetime. Now how on earth are we going to explain to our parents where we have been these past few days?”

“Silly Ferret, don’t you know anything about the space-time equilibrium? It’s not a question of how, but why for when?”

“Why for when?” parroted the bewildered knight of Bebounty.

“Yup, why for when” repeated the cheeky Major Commando Mega Jumbo as he took of his clothes revealing a bright orange bathing suite. “Time to go take a dip in the sea, are you coming sis?”

“Right behind you doofus” echoed Sherry. “Are you coming Ferris?”

Ferris was left utterly confused. Why were his two cousins so calm? So composed? He looked over towards that same living room clock that he was carefully studying the second they decided to blow their giant bubbles that got them past the TV and into Super Duper Land. Ferris was delighted to be amazed once more.

The time was still 10:10am.

THE END

www.ingramcontent.com/pod-product-compliance
Lightning Source LLC
LaVergne TN
LVHW091324150826
845673LV00006B/1754

* 9 7 9 8 6 6 1 2 7 0 3 6 8 *